"Tell me you didn't enjoy our kiss."

She crossed her arms and looked away.

Outside the reception doors now, Pace pulled up. When he didn't speak or let her down, she warily met his gaze.

"I'm sorry," he said. "Did you say something?"

She wanted to tell him to show a little mercy and let her go.

But, more, she wanted the achingly delicious sensation he whipped up inside her to go on. Seriously, if he could kiss like that, how would the rest of his repertoire pan out? How would it be to know Pace fully unleashed and acting purely on animal instinct? If he couldn't set her fireworks off, no one could.

Phoebe held her breath, curled her toes, then surrendered to a defeated sigh.

She looped arms around his neck and raised herself to meet his mouth. For better or worse, she was ready to start talking.

One Christmas long ago, **ROBYN GRADY** received a book from her big sister and immediately fell in love with Cinderella. Sprinklings of magic, deepest wishes come true—she was hooked! Picture books with glass slippers later gave way to romance novels and, more recently, the real-life dream of writing for Harlequin Books.

After a fifteen-year career in television, Robyn met her own modern-day hero. They live on Australia's Sunshine Coast, with their three little princesses, two poodles and a cat called Tinkie. She loves new shoes, worn jeans, lunches at Moffat Beach and hanging out with her friends on eHarlequin. Learn about her latest releases at www.robyngrady.com and don't forget to say hi. She'd love to hear from you!

EVERY GIRL'S SECRET FANTASY
ROBYN GRADY

~ Rogues & Rebels ~

TORONTO • NEW YORK • LONDON
AMSTERDAM • PARIS • SYDNEY • HAMBURG
STOCKHOLM • ATHENS • TOKYO • MILAN • MADRID
PRAGUE • WARSAW • BUDAPEST • AUCKLAND

Recycling programs
for this product may
not exist in your area.

ISBN-13: 978-0-373-52791-5

EVERY GIRL'S SECRET FANTASY

First North American Publication 2010.

Copyright © 2010 by Robyn Grady.

This edition published by arrangement with Harlequin Books S.A.

For questions and comments about the quality of this book
please contact us at Customer_eCare@Harlequin.ca.

® and TM are trademarks of the publisher. Trademarks indicated with
® are registered in the United States Patent and Trademark Office, the
Canadian Trade Marks Office and in other countries.

www.eHarlequin.com

Printed in U.S.A.

Praise for
Robyn Grady

Devil in a Dark Blue Suit
"This is a fun, wildly romantic lovers-reunited
tale. Readers will root for this pair as the hero
realizes that only by coming to terms with the
past can he move his life forward."
—*RT Book Reviews*

Confessions of a Millionaire's Mistress
"This emotional journey features a feisty
heroine determined to have it all. It proves
an interesting journey as [the heroine] tries to
convince the hero he deserves the same thing."
—*RT Book Reviews*

Hired for the Boss's Bed
"Grady wonderfully captures feelings of love,
envy, insecurity and ego in this terrific tale."
—*RT Book Reviews*

For Senior Editor extraordinaire
Kimberley Young

Thank you for your guidance and unfailing belief
in my work, for the amazing opportunities and,
most of all, your friendship.

CHAPTER ONE

KNEES gone weak, Phoebe Moore drank in the sight of two bronzed arms angling down over a well-packed T-shirt and large masculine hands raising its black interlock hem. Unaware of his company, the man dragged the shirt up over his head. At the same time Phoebe's throat thickened and her mouth went bone-dry. After a criminally toned abdomen and broad chest were revealed, he bunched the shirt into a ball and set about towelling all that premium meat and muscle.

Phoebe released a quivering sigh.

No wonder Brodricks Prestige Cars' slogan was "The Thrill of Your Life".

Dynamic, charming, all gloriously packaged in the body of a sex god, the man in question—the delectable Pace Davis—was Brodricks' lead technical adviser and resident chief mechanic. That chest, those jeans... The vision standing before her was enough to reduce Phoebe to a creamy puddle. But the best part—as well as the worst—was his sultry air of mystery. The three times she and Pace had met he'd seemed interested in details of her life, but had been curiously elusive about his own.

She could guess why.

At the far end of the otherwise deserted Sydney workshop, Pace swiped the shirt down one trunk of an arm and up the other. As he gave his delectably dewy chest another chamois, sensing a presence, he glanced over and gifted her a smile—a particularly sensual lopsided grin. Air eased from Phoebe's lungs as, moving to join her, Pace ruffled his inky-black hair into a tousled style.

That was how he'd look in the mornings, she decided, hugging her clip-folder close. Slightly dishevelled and completely desirable.

When the heat racing through her veins pooled and contracted low in her belly, Phoebe hauled herself back and drew up tall. Time to remember how late she'd stayed up the previous night making that list—her dare-to-be-bold, nothing-left-out wish list. The first point was underlined in red:

Reclaim my sexuality... Find Mr Right Now!

In one sense, dreamy Pace Davis was the perfect candidate. The friction that zapped between them would explode like two sticks of lit dynamite if they ever transferred their physical attraction to the bedroom. But taking that plunge with Pace would never happen, and for three very good reasons.

Phoebe tried to remember those reasons now, as Pace's electric blue gaze combed her shoulders, her hips, while that mouthwatering bare chest rolled to a stop a mere foot away. His eyes locked on hers, and his square jaw shifted before that rich, deep voice rumbled out.

"Well, well, if it isn't Miss Phoebe Moore." His brows swooped together. "But wait...there's something different about you."

Phoebe's face flushed hot. Different? Was it the spot on her chin?

"It's there in your eyes," he went on, and that wicked smile curved his mouth again. "It's finally happened. You've had a change of heart and want me to take you home."

Perhaps it was that honey-over-gravel voice, the smouldering intensity in his eyes, or the basic shocking truth in that line that almost undid her. Actually, it was all three—but no way would she tell Pace Davis that.

The first and biggest reason she wasn't going there with Pace was due to the fact they knew each other through work. After a failed office affair, Phoebe was acutely aware of the pitfalls that could follow mixing business with pleasure. Pace Davis, on the other hand, suffered no such reservation. On the first night they'd met, at a sponsorship cocktail party, he'd been dressed in a tuxedo and with seduction on his mind. He'd let her know with his eyes and subtle gestures that he wanted her. More to the point, he intended to have her. It was simply a matter of time.

Or so he thought.

Finding her strength, Phoebe lifted her chin. "No change of heart, Pace." She managed a casual shrug. "I don't think you're what I need right now."

Tipping close, his warm breath stirred her hair. "Wouldn't it be fun to find out for sure?"

When he rocked back, sexual awareness tugged her along like the drag from the *Starship Enterprise*. But Phoebe dug in her heels and reminded herself of the *second* reason she refused to cross that line with this near irresistible man.

Aside from Brodricks Prestige Cars having corporate connections with Goldmar Studios, the production house she worked for, Pace was a player…the kind of instinctively seductive male who didn't need to brag about his exploits but made no excuses for pursuing and then enjoying what he caught. The night they'd met he'd been lapping up the company of a gaggle of admiring women. She'd bet the only reason he'd lost interest in the others and set his sights on her was because she hadn't batted her lashes and immediately fallen at his feet. The second time they'd met, at a similar function, it had been the same story. Lots of women hanging off his every word. Pace in his element. That was evidence enough for her.

Certainly if she followed her list and found "Mr Right Now" she would be embarking on an intimate relationship with someone who may or may not be The One, but taking control of your fate was a far cry from agreeing to become another notch on some playboy's bedpost. The latter scenario cut way too close to the mistake her mother had made, and had ultimately paid dearly for.

Her young daughter, too.

On the other hand…Pace was certainly amusing, and a bit of harmless teasing never hurt anyone.

"I guess it *would* be fun to find out," she admitted, and when his blue eyes flashed added sweetly, "You'll be the first to know if I change my mind."

No smile this time. Rather, he stepped into her personal space and, when her neck tipped back, angled his head achingly close to hers. The heat of his body burrowed into her skin, making her tingle and feel entirely, dangerously out of her depth.

"Know what I love about you, Phoebe?" he growled in a low, entrancing voice that sent her heart and mind racing. "Your ability to avoid the unavoidable."

Flames licked up her limbs, across her breasts, over and between her legs. Pace's potency this minute was so close, so lethal, she could barely get enough air. Another few seconds—another inch or two—and his mouth would drop over hers. Time to get back on track, before the scrap of sanity she still possessed snapped and she surrendered completely.

Siphoning in a quiet breath, she slid one foot back—enough to put adequate distance between them and shortcircuit the sizzling connection.

"The desk manager said I'd find you out here." She was thankful her voice wasn't thick. "I've come to collect my car."

A measure of light flickered back up in his darkened eyes before he relented and slowly drew away. With a languid stride, he headed for a row of lockers. Game over...for the moment.

"Ah, yes," he said, stuffing the black T-shirt into a locker. "Your new 6 Series coupé. A contemporary beauty, with a world of simmering power just begging to be released."

She grinned at his subtext as he flicked her a devilish look and retrieved a fresh white replacement. After he'd slipped the shirt over his head and covered his CinemaScope chest, she sussed out the shop. So where *was* the BMW? She checked her watch. The sponsorship agreement said five p.m.

"I have the right date, don't I?"

"Don't worry," he told her. "We're not reneging on our agreement. Along with the advertising dollars we spend with your network, the president of the company is eager to provide a Brodricks prestige vehicle for the star of Goldmar Productions' latest ratings winner for personal use for one year." But then he cocked his head and gave his ear a tug. "Unfortunately we learned late this afternoon we won't have the car until Monday."

Phoebe's heart fell.

Perfect. Because of this deal she'd gone ahead and advertised her own early model car. It had gone to its new owners this morning. If she didn't have the sponsorship vehicle, she was without wheels. No problem normally, but this weekend it mattered.

A lot.

She took her thumbnail from her mouth. "What time Monday?"

A half-serious line creased his brow. "Were you planning on taking an extended test drive this weekend?"

Something like that. "I need to get to my hometown tomorrow. It's a speck on the map." And a six-hour round trip from Sydney.

Her Aunt Meg was due back from her most recent overseas jaunt, and the home Phoebe had shared with her, from the time of her mother's death until her big move to Sydney eight years ago, needed a small but crucial repair job.

Her aunt breezed through something like co-ordinating a two-month trek across Asia, yet suffered blatant uninterest in organising inconsequential domestic affairs—like avoiding frostbite when the temperature plummeted below zero. The town's only worthwhile handyman was teed up to fit a replacement part in the house boiler tomorrow. The evening weather was already chilly. If she didn't see to it before the real cold set in, no one would.

Pace had made himself comfortable, propped up against a nearby Alfa Romeo's door, arms and ankles crossed. "No problem," he said. "I'll organise a loaner."

"Really?" Phoebe sparked up. "Could I pick it up tomorrow, some time after noon?"

He winked. "Leave it with me."

Problem solved and business concluded, she thanked the Brodricks representative for his time, then promptly turned for the wide garage door, which led to the offices and main exit.

"Hey, hold up a minute."

At his call—mellow and embracing, like an offshore breeze on a summer's day—Phoebe rotated back.

"Need a lift home?" he said, pushing off the car door. "Don't like your chances of finding a cab this time of day."

Butterflies were released in her stomach at the thought of sharing a ride—just the two of them, sitting close, completely alone. The idea made her insides contract with longing and her breathing come a little quicker, but she shook off the notion and sent a cool smile.

"Thanks. I'll be fine."

A crooked grin stole across his face as those big shoulders rolled toward her. "Maybe we could stop for a coffee on the way. I'd offer a sample from the workshop percolator, but I'd rather you left here alive."

He arched a brow at a suspect glass pot, which might have been brewing since last Christmas.

When a small laugh escaped, Phoebe quickly bit her lip. "I honestly don't think—"

"How about you leave the thinking to me?" In full seductive mode again, he strolled closer. "And *I* think you can't be in that big of a rush." A sultry look burned in his eyes. "Or do you have a special night planned?"

"Only with my Lhasa Apso."

"Lucky dog." His mischievous grin might have been envious. "But I'm sure the pooch won't mind if you're a few minutes late."

On a scale of difficulty, it was on a par with applying double-sided cleavage tape, but Phoebe managed to crimp her mouth into a flippant *thanks-but-no-thanks* smile and spin on her heel.

With a parting, "I'll be in tomorrow to collect the car," she headed out through the door.

She was right to deflect Pace's advances. Although, truth be told, experiencing the full extent of his blistering brand of passion could almost be worth getting burned...particularly considering her last lukewarm experience with a man.

Instant attraction had bitten deep the day she'd met her boss, a year ago. Steve Trundy was tall and blond, with muscles that gleamed like polished steel after one of his regular workouts. She didn't know a woman at Goldmar's who didn't want to date him. When he'd asked her out, Phoebe had melted and murmured yes.

Their first all-out attempt at passion had been after hours, in an unmanned studio control room. Embarrassingly less than successful. Phoebe had blamed the malfunction on her worry over someone walking in and catching them out, so when Steve had suggested a romantic weekend away she'd leapt at the chance. But the niggling she'd experienced in the control room that night had surfaced again.

She'd been baffled. Steve was intelligent, attractive, *built*. The lack of stimulation had to be her fault, not his. Surely next time would be different?

Willing to let the emotion and enthusiasm grow, she'd persevered, showing him what she liked in the bedroom and trying her best to please him too. But little had improved and there had come a point where she'd begun to avoid situations that might lead to intimacy. She'd thought she was in love with him, but how could that be when she shied away almost every time he touched her?

After nine months two weeks and three days, she'd broken down and, cheeks flaming, admitted that something vital was missing. The connection—the hunger—that should be there simply wasn't. She'd felt so bad. She'd begged Steve not to blame himself.

He hadn't. In fact he'd puffed up his chest and lost no time insisting that, if she wanted to know, he didn't much enjoy sleeping with *her* either. She was so tense and staid, he said. *Boring* was another word he'd used. He was sorry too…that she was sexually dysfunctional. When her back had gone up and she'd defended herself he'd less than kindly pointed out that a raging inferno drowning in jet fuel couldn't spark her match.

She could have shaken off the insult, which was obviously the result of a dented ego, if only she didn't have to see Steve and his jilted face five days a week at the studios. When they were in the same room, his "frigid" accusation played over in her mind and icicles would form, freezing solid in her veins. But there was nothing wrong with her. They simply weren't sexually compatible. It happened.

Still, as more time went by and Phoebe looked back on her romantic past, she began to wonder if Steve might to some degree be right. She'd had intimate relationships before, but not many, and she'd never enjoyed the volcanic, lose-your-mind, cry-out-his-name kind of lovemaking that she knew must exist.

Sitting alone in her apartment last night, she'd decided she'd spent long enough torturing herself over it. It was time to act! Her doubts needed to be washed away—and not with a few trickles but a downpour. With no truly memorable sexual experiences to speak of, at twenty-six she needed to know that she was capable of being consumed by the mindless fever that went hand-in-hand with heart-pounding, out-of-this-world, give-me-more sex. She'd read about that kind of explosive euphoria—had even dreamed of it a few times. Other women found it.

Why not her?

But brazen bad boy Pace wasn't the answer, as tempting as succumbing might be. Not only was that man a lesson in heartbreak waiting to happen, what if the unthinkable happened? What if she was wrong and Steve was right and she *wasn't* capable of feeling the earth move, or seeing a thousand stars go off in her head? Tanking with Steve had been uncomfortable. But she'd coped.

Pace was another matter.

Now whenever Pace looked at her all she could see, all she could feel, was his barely contained desire. It sizzled over her, drew her in and made her feel as if she were some kind of goddess. If she slept with Pace and they failed to lift off, that smouldering attention would be replaced with something a whole lot less flattering... like disappointment. Or, worse, pity.

Shuddering, Phoebe walked faster.

No way. Not with Pace. She'd be humiliated into the next decade. That was the third and strongest reason she must stay well away.

Phoebe moved through the massive Brodricks show-room, its vast glass walls encasing a dazzling parade of gleaming vehicles that movie stars and Arab sheikhs might drive. Bentley, Ferrari, Rolls-Royce... She hated to guess how much this place was insured for. How must it feel to be that insanely rich? Like the vast majority of the world, she'd never know.

Outside a moment later, the early-evening air was brisk, with the crush of autumn leaves littering the pavement. Busy pedestrians swirled all around, and overhead deepening shades of blue had drawn up a blanket, preparing to tuck in for the night.

Her hand high, she hailed an approaching cab. Along with a fleet of other peak-hour traffic, it sailed by. So did a second and a third cab. Five long minutes later, when she spotted a fourth cruising down Botany Road, she shot out an arm and waved a giant arc. The cab slowed down. Smiling and waving again, she moved forward. She didn't see the motorbike zipping in to stop ahead of the cab. Didn't notice its helmeted rider...at least not until he reached out from his perch at the kerb to lay a steely grip on her arm.

She scowled. *What the hell?*

"Get your hands *off* me," she growled, wrenching her arm free. "What do you think you're doing?"

The first bell to ring was the white T-shirt, visible

under the rider's open leather jacket. The second, when the visor flipped up, was that delicious *don't-you-want-me?* smile. The voice—a warm summer breeze—came in a fatal third.

Pace Davis leaned back and revved his bike. "Actually, I wondered if you'd changed your mind about that lift?"

"You?" Her mouth opened and closed twice before she got another word out. "I didn't know you rode a bike."

He removed the helmet and rubbed the dark, day-long bristles framing his wry smile. "For a few years now." He hitched forward. "Here…jump on."

"I—I don't double on bikes."

"You mean *don't* or never tried?"

An unbidden fire ripped through her system, and for one dizzy moment she imagined herself, novice thighs clinging to hot metal, arms gathering living granite, breasts crushed against comforting firm warmth. The mere thought of being that close to definitely-off-limits made her sway a little and lose her breath.

Cursing the blush rising in her cheeks, she hurried on. "Either way, it doesn't matter. I have a cab waiting."

She gestured to…a vacant space.

Shifting her gaze, she spotted her taxi merging into the traffic with a passenger in the back seat. At this rate she'd never get home. Her attention slid back to Pace and her heartbeat thumped at his focused gaze. She shook her head slowly.

"This is not a good idea."

"I'm not kidnapping you. It's only a lift."

Sure. That was why mischief was twinkling like rough diamonds in his eyes.

"Oh, come on," he teased. "Live a little. I guarantee you'll enjoy the ride. Bet my best wrench on it."

Lateral thinking sent her head spinning at the prospect of winning this man's prize tool.

Phoebe evaluated her attire…a cream bandage dress cut above the knee, five-inch gladiator sandal heels. How could she consider straddling that steed in *this* get-up?

A challenging smile lifted one side of his mouth. "Don't think, Phoebe. Just do."

Her gaze dropped from his entrancing blue eyes to his come-kiss-me lips. The smell of grease mingled with a hard day's work and a faint tang of aftershave—something woodsy and distinctly memorable—and wrapped itself around her hypersensitive skin. Thoughts about possible embarrassment drifted away. He was right. She was overreacting. If she accepted this ride it would mean nothing more than a lift on a busy afternoon.

And yet she couldn't help but look forward to clinging to his back, to moulding her hands over biceps that must be carved from rock. He would be so hot, so hard…more scrumptious than she'd ever dreamed.

Reading her mind, Pace widened his smile before he made the decision for her. Relieving her of the folder, he slid it into a slimline compartment on the bike's side. Accepting the fact that every one of her marbles had suffered a major meltdown, Phoebe caught the spare helmet, took his hand, and swung a leg up and over the smooth seat behind the rider. The motor roared as he gunned the throttle and she set the strap under her chin.

"Now, hold on tight," he said as the visor dropped into place. "*Real* tight."

And she did, unable to hold back a whooping laugh as they shot out into a break in traffic.

Phoebe Moore could be summed up in two words.

SEX. EE.

Reaffirming that truth, Pace leaned his machine into a corner and sweet Phoebe cuddled in close. Feminine fingers clutched, warm thighs pinched, and firm breasts pushed. Smiling, he gunned the throttle for an extra burst of speed.

No contest. This woman grew more alluring each time they met. She was cute, though not ditsy. Sassy, yet kind of shy. Open, but not overbearing. Hell, she was a whole lot of things. In other words, he wanted her. And, despite driving him crazy with an impressive array of excuses, the truth of the matter sparkled in her eyes.

She wanted him too.

Pace deciphered Phoebe's flailing arm directions and slid into a vacant space outside the well-situated northside apartment block. Slanting his long legs down to steady the stationary bike, Pace felt his heartbeat slip into third as Phoebe wiggled free of her mount. Smoothing down the skirt hitched up on those heavenly hips, she removed the helmet and shook out a satiny stream of pale blonde hair. He'd dreamed of that hair. Tonight he planned to touch it.

"Thanks for the lift." Phoebe handed back the spare helmet with an exuberant smile. "I must admit…it was fun."

A heavy throb condensed in the pit of his stomach at the thought of all the fun they *would* have.

He shot a casual glance around the mix of suburban weatherboards and trendy complexes huddled between towering gum trees. No graffiti. Buckets of kids. Nearby, someone had removed what smelled like a lamb roast from the oven.

"Nice neighbourhood," he said, meeting her gaze again.

"I was lucky to get a place so close to the city that's almost reasonable in rent." She nodded at the adjacent park. "There's barbecue areas and swings close for families. Alfresco restaurants and a mall down the road, too. It's a good combination. Pretty and full of possibilities."

Drinking her smile in, Pace felt his blood simmer. *It certainly is.*

Bringing himself back, he glanced over his shoulder. "We passed a Japanese restaurant on the way in."

Phoebe's eyes flashed with approval. "I eat there all the time. It's the freshest in town. Their rainbow rolls are to die for and—" She stopped, her head tilting as though she were embarrassed or disappointed with herself. "Sushi isn't everyone's favourite."

"I'm an atmosphere man," he confirmed. "If the service is good, lighting right and the company special…" He pictured them in a darkened corner, touching, kissing, and eased into a grin. "Well, I'm usually on my way to being satisfied."

Her eyebrows gradually knitted. "Satisfied…" she murmured, then, "I can imagine you'd want to be."

Pace frowned. The luminance in her glittering jade gaze was fading, eclipsed by that familiar, infuriating restraint. When she took a step back on those sexy heels, as if yanked by an imaginary lead, he almost spilled off his bike.

"You're leaving?"

"I've kept you long enough." She smiled her dimpled smile and turned away. "Thanks for the lift."

As she swept up the paved steps, disappearing into the building without a backward glance, Pace grinned to himself. If she wanted to play impossible to get, he'd simply get more inventive. He liked a challenge. In fact, he'd been raised on them.

And he always won.

Well, almost always.

Kicking up the stand, Pace prepared to pull out into the next break. At the same time the cellphone on his belt vibrated. Ditching the helmet, he studied the ID and groaned. It was the weekend, for crying out loud. What did his brother want now?

Actually, his *half*-brother. His father had married soon after his first wife had died in childbirth. His second marriage had produced another son. In a perfect world the two brothers might have become inseparable. Instead Pace and the slightly older Nicholas Junior had grown up at loggerheads, competing at everything, including their busy father's attention, each step of the way. As grown men, nothing much had changed.

Setting his jaw, Pace thumbed a button and connected. "Hey, Nick."

Nick didn't bother with pleasantries. "Have you addressed the consignment arrival problem for that Bugatti? I need to know by eleven Monday morning. No later."

Nick would still be sitting at his big desk, surrounded

by paperwork, dark hair spiked from numerous run-throughs with his hand. In his absolute element.

"Hello? Anyone there?"

Pace grated his back teeth. "I'm here."

"You could show a little more interest," Nick growled, and Pace growled back.

"And you could quit with the attitude."

"There's something wrong with wanting to get things done and done right?"

Steam rose beneath his leather collar, but Pace kept his response to an almost civil warning. "Nick, don't go there."

He could do without the thinly veiled reminders.

Five years ago Pace had taken on the presidential seat of the family business, Brodricks Prestige Cars, but not because he was partial to reams of figures and boardroom meetings. After his father's death, his will had left Pace in charge. The younger son had seen the promotion as a responsibility he couldn't shirk, even when Nick, the brother with the accounting skills and economics letters behind his name, had made it clear he was the best man for the job. Pace, a practical rather than academic type, with an engineering background, wasn't sure he disagreed.

No secret—Pace had enjoyed the lifestyle his inheritance and position provided. He'd partied hard, had chalked up some amazing experiences, and had entertained some exceedingly attractive company. But there was a definite downside.

He was happiest when talking cars, analysing precision engines or test-driving the fastest, classiest automobiles in the world—Jaguar, McLarens, Mercedes, Porsche—vehicles available for sale or lease through

Brodricks. Design and hands-on tasks were where he excelled. Being locked behind a desk during working hours was far from his ideal existence. It had shown—not only in his demeanour but more tellingly in Brodricks' books which, after his first two years at the helm, hadn't looked nearly as healthy as they should. The final straw had come when he'd made a couple of glaring errors regarding funds in a foreign investment account.

At the subsequent board meeting to analyse the extent of the damage he'd maintained a firm chin, but had secretly wanted the floor to open up and swallow him whole. Hell, it wasn't as if he'd *asked* for the job. He'd been too young—too full of juice—for the conservative life of a suit. His father should have considered that instead of constantly pushing. All concerned would have been far better off if he'd stuck to what he did best and left the tricky, aka *boring* bits to others.

Of course Nick had agreed.

With a handshake and a smirk his half-brother had stepped up, while Pace, needing to dodge unwanted media attention, had taken on an alias and spent the next two years overseas, incognito, researching premium automobiles all over the globe. He'd come back to Australia pumped, and champing at the bit to reclaim control over the technical side of the business. But he'd got used to his new identity, and the screen it provided from the media radar, so he'd kept the twist on his name—Pace Davis, rather than Davis Pace Brodrick.

Nick maintained that their father had chosen the slightly younger son to head the company because Pace had been his favourite. But Nick refused to examine the more valid reason underpinning their father's decision.

Pace not only understood cars, he *lived* for them—like the old man had. And that was Pace's saving grace. Nick might be the current financial brain behind the name, but Pace was and would always be Brodricks' heart.

Which meant doing what was best for the company and, if at all possible, keeping his temper where his brother was concerned.

"I'll have that data to you first thing Monday," he ground out, and then, to change the subject, "How's Amy?"

Nick's fiancée was a sweetheart. Pace liked to hear she was well.

But Nick stayed on track. "Meeting's at eleven. I'll see you with the information at eight." The call disconnected.

Compressing his lips, but then letting a curse fly anyway, Pace slotted the cellphone back on its clip.

He and Nick had always been last-one-left-standing rivals and always would be. Their glove-to-chin history could never be erased. As much as he'd like to believe in fairytales, no way, no how, would he and Nick ever get along. Sorry truth was neither of them wanted to.

His helmet fitted, Pace switched his thoughts to a more pleasant matter…his budding relationship with the scintillating Phoebe Moore. Given her clear-cut departure moments ago, sadly getting to know Phoebe on more intimate terms would have to wait until another time.

After a late model Merc had hummed by, Pace revved his engine and swung out. Then, like a godsend, he remembered that folder lying safe and sound in the bike's compartment near his thigh. Beneath his helmet a wide smile broke. Catching a break in the oncoming traffic, he lunged into a knee-to-road one-eighty.

Seemed Lady Luck was on his side.

CHAPTER TWO

PHOEBE opened her apartment door, dropped her bag, and crossed to her cosy living room. After thumbing on a side-lamp, she fell like a bowling pin into the chintz couch.

What a ride!

What would Roz Morelli do when she learned her best friend had been whisked away upon the throbbing axis of a gorgeous man's bike? Scream with envy, that was what. Phoebe could barely believe it herself.

After hugging onto that broad leather-clad back all the way home, her mind was filled with an assortment of intoxicating images. Closing her eyes, she saw Pace's spectacular body—not sitting before her on that bike but poised above her, his big bare biceps either side of her head, his lidded gaze conveying a message that needed no words. She imagined his soft, skilled lips brushing hers, his deft wet tongue pushing inside, and that kernel of longing blooming at her core glowed brighter still.

Milking the delicious syrupy feeling, she held onto the vision a scrumptious moment more, then reluctantly forced her eyes open and reached for the list she'd left on the side table the night before. She scanned the lines, then zoned back in on item number one: *Find Mr Right Now.*

She'd decided Pace couldn't be the one. They were connected through work. He was obviously a playboy. And, perhaps worst of all…

She shuddered.

What if they failed to launch in the bedroom? How hard would it be to accept that even with someone of Pace's calibre she bombed out beneath the sheets? Worse, whenever they met she'd have to face *his* disappointment as well as her own. Pace was a man who would expect satisfaction in all aspects of his life— particularly, she suspected, when enjoying himself with the opposite sex. After the near-ruthless way he'd pursued her, the idea of ultimately turning Pace *off* rather than *on* left her cringeing to her toes.

No matter how much he tampered with her temperature when they were in flirting mode, nothing guaranteed that would translate into a success story when they were naked and heart-thumpingly alone. It was hard enough facing Steve, reliving his words and the embarrassment every time she saw him. She refused to risk going through the same wretchedness whenever she and Pace met. The risk wasn't worth it. It was much wiser, much safer, to keep the fantasy of *what if?* alive for them both.

Three sharp raps sounded on her door. Phoebe found her feet and, after a second to think it through, a smile. Must be Mrs G.

Her neighbour and landlady was a brash old thing, who smelled of seventies cologne and soft-serve ice cream. But she adored Hannie, Phoebe's dog. Given the time she spent at work, Phoebe was grateful for

Mrs G's eagerness to puppysit. For convenience's sake, her neighbour had her own key to let herself in and out of Phoebe's apartment. However, understanding of another's privacy, Mrs G always knocked first.

But when Phoebe fanned back the door the breath caught in her throat. A heartbeat later the strength in her legs drained like water from up-ended bottles. Not Mrs G. With one shoulder propped against the jamb, and the sort of casual, sexy attitude that was always inherent, never learned, Pace Davis stood in her doorway.

One dark brow arched over a crooked grin. *"Surprise."*

Her gaze flew from his teasing eyes to the folder visible in one large tanned hand. "Ohmi...I totally forget—"

"Your folder." He straightened to his full six-foot-plus height. "Thought you might need it."

The folder contained a rundown for tomorrow's *SLAMM* recording. She went cold thinking of Steve's snide reaction should word get back that she'd shown up at the studio less than prepared. Since their breakup Steve had turned over any rock that might help provide him with a reason to dismiss her. He hated being reminded of their failed relationship. He'd much prefer her gone.

Phoebe accepted the folder from Pace. "Thank you." She remembered the lift home and her smile deepened. "Again."

"Well, I happened to be in the neighbourhood," he joked. "Saw your light on..."

He looked so strong, so unaccountably attractive, every glorious wonderful inch of him. But it was his eyes that drew Phoebe most. So alive and compelling. So startlingly blue and intense.

As if sensing her slide, he edged a fraction closer. That beguiling scent stole into her lungs, and something primal tugged in the base of her tummy. Shrinking back, Phoebe hauled herself in. She'd better get rid of him before she did something impulsive that they both might live to regret.

She summoned up a breezy smile. "So, guess I'll see you when I collect my car tomorrow."

"After midday. I'll be there." Pace set one hand high on the jamb. "You're recording your show in the morning?" When she nodded, he grinned. "*SLAMM*. Should be the name of a basketball show. What does it stand for again?"

Phoebe hid a grin. He knew darn well what the letters stood for. He simply wanted to hear her say it. She wouldn't give him the satisfaction of blushing.

"It stands for *Sex, Love and Maybe Marriage*. We invite couples on the show who are in a relationship, in love, and thinking of making it legal."

"Ah, yes. I remember now. It's all there in the sponsorship file. I really ought to catch a recording some time."

"Let me know when. I'm sure the producer will look after you."

When he inclined his head, light from her side-lamp caught his eyes, making them glitter like cut-crystal. "I was hoping *you'd* look after me."

Phoebe quietly held her stomach. There went that addictive tug in her belly again. It wasn't that she didn't *want* to look after him. Even now it would be so easy to invite him in, offer a drink, let the evening unfold and ultimately give in to this maddening desire to kiss him.

Kiss him and more.

Nearby, a muffled tinkling peeled out. Brought back, and feeling a little light-headed, she glanced around. Her bag was ringing.

Muttering, "Excuse me…" Phoebe dropped and rummaged around. But at the exact moment she found the cell in her bag the ringtone stopped. A couple of seconds later a text message was available.

Call back NOW!
Steve

Phoebe moaned.

What was she supposed to have done now?

"Bad news?" Pace asked, folding down beside her.

"To put it mildly."

"Looks like you need a distraction." His gaze dipped to trace the line of her mouth and a telling warmth swirled through her middle. "Grab your coat," he prodded. "Come out with me."

Phoebe gripped the phone. Her fingers ached to brush that raspy jaw. They also itched to ring Steve back and tell him to quit being such a baby, to grow up and use some manners. She was tired of showing up for work wondering what low comment Steve might have for her. She wished she could think of a way to fix the problem, but she wasn't about to leave the job she adored. Steve wasn't going anywhere either.

Mixing business with pleasure…

Her gaze roamed Pace's handsome, expectant face and she pushed to her feet.

She wouldn't make that mistake twice.

She shook her head. "Pace, let's not do this."

He rolled back those shoulders. The intensity of his determination was palpable.

"I want to try something," he said, in a take-no-prisoners tone. "I want you to touch me."

Phoebe backed up, horrified. *Tempted.*

Touch him? She couldn't. She *wouldn't*.

Her eyes popped.

Oh, God. He was winding out of his jacket!

"Don't bother making excuses," he said. "I was right about the lift, wasn't I? You were worried about nothing. You enjoyed the ride."

She honed in on the definition of his chest, discernible through the shirt, and when her slack mouth refused to work she licked her suddenly dry lips and willed her voice not to crack.

"Th-that was different."

"No difference." His jacket dropped and buckles pinged on the floor. "Promise."

Her cheeks felt on fire. Her legs were all wobbly and dangerously weak. She wanted to recoil. Show him that she was serious and that this time he'd gone too far.

"I don't see that this has anything to do with—"

She was cut off when she found her hand, small and pliable, engulfed in his.

His brows fell together. "I'll tell you what this has to do with. You accepting that we're attracted to each other. That's nothing to be ashamed of. Nothing to be worried about. I don't have a criminal record. I'm not a Jekyll and Hyde. Take this one little step, Phoebe. If you feel uncomfortable I'll leave and never mention it again. You have my word."

Entranced, Phoebe stood, trapped in his eyes.

Crazy...*foolish*...but she believed him.

More importantly, there was a way to work this standoff to her advantage.

She could go along with this game, and if she didn't melt not only would Pace back off from now on, but her curiosity in that department would also be satisfied. She'd wanted to sample more intimate contact with Pace without the risk of embarrassing herself. This was her chance. It didn't mean she had to go any further if she didn't want to.

Or *he* didn't.

After a deliberating moment she nodded, and let him place her palm on his chest.

Immediately a delicious buzz sped through her body. Her insides contracted and her eyes drifted shut.

Heat.

Rock.

Very...very...nice...

She heard her own sigh and, caught out, let her eyes fly open. He was looking down at her, completely in control. Annoyingly superior. What must it feel like to know you were just that good?

Snatching her hand away, she hoisted up her chin and croaked, "Satisfied?"

"We're not finished."

His roughened hands caught both of hers and held them firmly against his hard chest again. His piercing gaze seemed to search her soul. "Now put your cheek on mine."

A world of alarm bells went off.

"I *can't*," she cried while his hot hands kneaded hers. Could she? *Should* she?

"Give me one reason why not," he said, a hypnotic smile shining in his eyes.

"You're…" She licked her lips again while her heartbeat boomed. Finally she murmured, "You're too tall."

He grinned. Bent lower. "Your cheek, Phoebe. Here on mine."

His deep voice vibrated beyond her fingers, booming a breathless path through the channels of her mind and her body. She'd come this far. If she didn't go further, even a little, she would always wonder.

Carefully she craned her neck. Her face touched his, that wonderful scent spilled through her system, the tips of her fingers tingled and the room began a slow spin.

Eyelids growing heavy, she instinctively rubbed her cheek up. He, in response, grazed his down. She dissolved as a smouldering pulse leapt to life between her legs and dragged another sigh from her throat.

Sandpaper scuffed near her ear when his chin dipped around. Noses brushed—once, twice—before his slightly parted lips dusted hers. Overtaken by sensation, she trembled to her socks when his deep, rich voice hummed against her left temple.

"I'm right about this, Phoebe. Right about us."

The moist, heaven-sent kiss that lingered on her brow dropped an airy veil of longing upon her shoulders. He moved back and she trembled, waiting for those lips. Waiting for that kiss. Waiting…

Waiting?

Her eyes shot open, and the wonderful fuzzy feeling evaporated like six p.m. cocktails.

The door was wide open, but Pace, and his leather jacket, were gone.

CHAPTER THREE

BY A quarter to twelve the following day, *SLAMM* had finished its Saturday morning recording.

The floor manager was ushering out the chattering audience. Overhead, banks of lights were fading down. Soon the crew would disassemble and move the set to scenery. And in the back row of the bleachers a patient Pace Davis sat and watched and waited.

Out of sight, anxious and hidden in the wings, Phoebe curled her fingers around the studio floor curtain and rolled her teeth over her bottom lip. She hadn't noticed until halfway through the morning that Pace had followed up on his suggestion of the day before. He'd come in to see for himself how a television show was recorded, and had left her seriously off balance in the process.

When she hadn't been in front of the camera she'd watched him from the wings, as she did now. Was it her imagination? Or had he indeed been distracted a great deal of the time, absorbed in his thoughts, and not pleasant ones. But whenever their gazes had meshed over the heads of the energised audience crowd, his vibrancy had faded back up and her limbs had turned to jelly. Amazing. Even in this very public environment, surrounded by hundreds of people, her reaction to his presence was something perilously close to overwhelming. Given the steady gleam in his eye, she wondered if he planned to play another of his games, and this time claim the kiss he'd left behind last night.

Swallowing against the nerves jumping in her throat, Phoebe watched as Pace pushed to his feet and looked expectantly around. She'd been upset last night when he'd left her standing, waiting, in her doorway. No, upset wasn't the word. She'd been livid.

Every time they met he openly pursued her—let her know that he'd like nothing better than to take her to his bed. Yesterday he'd had the perfect opportunity to push that point a long way towards home. She'd been ready and shamelessly willing to kiss him. The question was…if that kiss had been a wild success, would she have risked going further? Had she been at that point where mindless passion would have superseded inhibition and taken over?

He affected her so deeply. She'd barely slept last night for reliving every thrilling moment of that bike ride home and then his showing up unexpectedly at her door. She'd tossed and turned and wondered a thousand times what would have happened if instead of leaving he'd leaned in and pressed his lips hungrily to hers. And every time she wondered, her belly would heat and throb with longing.

Just like now.

But she couldn't stand here flustering all day.

Sucking it up, Phoebe stepped out from behind the curtain and willed Pace's sweeping gaze to meet hers. When he spotted her his eyes flashed, and the sexy grin that never failed to fling her pulse-rate up into overdrive curved one corner of his mouth.

Instantly entranced, Phoebe smiled back as a warm and wonderful fever swept over her skin. Beneath the bodice of her pink silk blouse her breasts grew heavy and tingled at the tips. Her awakened body told her what her mind already knew…what she'd *always* known. No couple could predict with absolute certainty whether they would ultimately set off each other's fireworks behind closed doors, but, coming out of the gate, there was every indication that she and Pace would reach the finish line at a gallop.

Then again, she'd once thought the same about Steve, and look how that had turned out.

As Pace descended the audience steps, his gait fluid and purposeful, Phoebe held her freefalling stomach and inhaled a deep calming breath. She'd been determined never again to contaminate her work environment with matters of the heart. She'd set her mind never to make her mother's mistake and lay herself open to the manipulations of a bad boy, a man so confident and attractive and damnably sexy that once a woman allowed him into her life there was every chance she'd still be hooked long after the party was over. And yet, despite all the negatives, as he made his way over she could think of only one thing…

Picking up where she and the best of the bad boys had left off. Come what may, she wanted to know the soul-lifting sensation of his mouth covering hers while his hands on her shoulders drew her close. Already she could feel his palms edging her straps down, his touch moulding over her breasts, slipping beneath the elastic of her panties and then scooping between the receptive join of her inner thighs. Stroking her…loving her…

Overheated, Phoebe fanned herself with her run-down, then repositioned her bag strap firmly over her shoulder. This was getting way too hard and way too hot. The constant tug of war—whether she should or whether she shouldn't—was making her crazy. A mass of frazzled nerves.

The sooner she was out of here, away from Pace, and on her way to Tyler's Stream the better.

They met at the bottom of the bleachers amidst the smell of spilt soda, banks of dying lights and streams of departing audience members, who veered about them like rapids around two rocks. No surprise, Pace's smile—oblique and entrancing—held even more power now that he was within touching distance.

Kissing distance.

He settled his arms over that edible chest, which this morning was covered by a collared white shirt, sleeves rolled high enough to reveal prominent cords wreathed beneath the surface of bronzed forearms. Phoebe held back a sigh as her tummy muscles twinged and squeezed. Could this man look anything other than completely sexy?

Too late, Phoebe realised she was staring. From the satisfied slant of his smile Pace realised it too. Clearing her throat, her cheeks flushed, she dropped her gaze. But other women passing weren't shy about checking out the darkly attractive man who, remarkably, seemed to have eyes only for her.

Phoebe had a logical explanation for that.

She was his current object of desire. The power of the pre-coital gaze was well documented and part and parcel of any genuine seduction attempt. Predators mesmerised their prey with the power of their eyes. He was *supposed* to make her feel this warm and wickedly bothered...this giddy and aching with want inside.

Phoebe shook herself partway back. This was *so* not the time. So definitely not the place.

Herding her whirling thoughts together, she curled stray hair behind an ear and, schooling her expression, asked in a blithe tone, "So, how'd you like the show?"

"Very much." A frown creased his tanned brow. "But I'm glad it's over."

She blinked at him. Glad? "Really?"

He stepped closer. "It means you're free."

When he gifted her a smile meant to strip the clothes from her body Phoebe battled to contain any evidence that might reveal she was liquefying on the inside, and in an extremely pleasant way.

Instead she pointed out, "I won't be free for long. I have that trip home to make today, remember?"

"Indeed I do." He performed a flourishing wave in the general direction of the car park. "Madame, your ride awaits you."

Understanding dawned, and a soft smile lifted her mouth. He'd brought the loaner car here rather than have her go all the way into Brodricks. Bad boy or not, he was pretty good at this white knight stuff.

"I appreciate that," she said, her tone nothing but sincere.

"Perhaps you can do me a favour in return."

Her heart skipped several beats and, alert again, she laced then locked her fingers behind her back. "If it has anything to do with my hands touching your chest, count me out."

Not here anyway.

He chuckled. "Still in denial?"

She wasn't in denial. She knew the power he potentially had over her. Knew the dangers, too. But was *he* honest enough to be one hundred per cent truthful about what was behind his interest in her?

"Perhaps you can help me overcome my…*denial*," she said. "Why don't you tell me why you're so keen for us to be…to be…?"

"Lovers?" he supplied and, her heart hammering at the evocative image that word drew in her head, she nodded. He rolled back his shoulders. "All right. I will."

She had no time to think, to dodge, to tell him that what he was about to do was highly inappropriate—as if that would have stopped him. One second she was challenging him to admit that his persistence was more about the thrill of the chase than any extraordinary quality on her part except, perhaps, resistance. The next strong hands had cupped her bare shoulders and determined arms drew her near. Her heart had no time to leap from her chest before the event she'd imagined far too often was actually happening. And the reality of the experience was a thousand times more thrilling, and *devastating*, than she could ever have dreamed possible.

As his mouth met hers, a steam bath of longing rose up and stole the rest of her breath away. The effect started low in her belly and sped through her veins, making her every sense heat up and her mind go blank then bright with a million colours. She felt him, smelled him, and as his mouth locked over hers *tasted* him too, with every famished, sighing cell in her body.

He drew her closer at the same time as his tongue pried her lips apart.

But that wasn't true. No force was needed. She opened up for him, offering no struggle. No fight. Rather, she let the rundown slip from her grasp and, as if on autopilot, slid her palms up over the steely cage of his ribs, then higher to grip the velvet-covered rock available beneath the smooth fabric of his shirt. Her fingertips brushed and then kneaded the buttons, aching to rip the front wide open.

When all too soon his mouth gradually left hers, Phoebe's eyes remained closed and her clinging fingers stayed glued to his chest. She could feel his heart beating all the way through to her bones. His primal heat swirled out, filling her like a flash storm filled a needy well.

A deep, assured voice filtered through her pulsing fog. "Does that answer your question?"

Her heavy eyelids dragged open.

His strong shadowed jaw was the first thing she saw, but she felt so light-headed the world seemed to be tipped on its axis. Was she still on the same planet? In the same century?

Awareness slowly filtered back and, with an ice-cold draft falling through her middle, Phoebe realised precisely where she was. Then another even more frightening reality bubbled up.

Heat scorched her face as, near rigid with shame, she carefully angled her head. Her vision arced a horrifyingly slow forty-five degrees. The room was dead quiet, but not empty…in fact very much the opposite.

Perhaps fifty people stood frozen, all eyes on them. Some folk stared with mouths wide open. Others were grinning like loons. Many women held their hearts, a look of sublime amazement mixed with envy stamped on their faces.

Phoebe withered into her shoes as a shivering, shaky sensation dropped through her middle. Just when she thought she might shrivel up and keel over with embarrassment, a voice broke the silence.

"Mummy, that lady doesn't look so good. Maybe *Daddy* should give her mouth to mouth next?"

It was too much. Phoebe's knees gave way.

As she went to stabilise her weight against the bleachers' hand rail, Pace caught and swept her up into his arms. A unified sigh from the crowd went up around them. She was centre stage in a way she hadn't anticipated. Certainly didn't want. She hadn't *meant* to lose herself and kiss him back. She'd surrendered her senses in one very weak moment. Surrendered completely...

And enjoyed it—as everyone had no doubt seen.

Smothering a groan, she hid her face in her hands.

She'd made a display of herself in front of her workmates—in front of her *audience*—with the man who'd made no bones about declaring she shouldn't fight what compelled them together. Her cheeks felt like twin ovens, even as her body sizzled with the afterglow of the magic.

Even while she secretly wished that amazing kiss hadn't ended quite so soon.

Her flushed face still buried in her hands, she felt Pace set off with a languid gait. Soon the resumed noises of the crew cleaning up and the audience leaving through the studio side exit faded. When she had the courage to come out from her hideyhole Pace was strolling through Goldmar's enormous front reception area, cradling her in his arms as if she weighed no more that a bag full of feathers.

Behind her circular polished teak desk, Cheryl the receptionist sat up for a better look as Pace marched them across the crimson-carpeted expanse. From the surrounding walls the eyes of the studio's "stars" peered down at them. Phoebe hadn't got used to seeing her own face up there yet. When Steve Trundy heard about this incident he'd want to set a new record in ripping it down.

Pace stopped in front of her giant close-up and angled his head, analysing. "It's a good print, but it doesn't capture your...effervescence."

With Cheryl's interest still firmly upon them, Phoebe didn't need to discuss photography. But Pace studied the shot more keenly, before dropping his gaze to search her features. "Your eyes sparkle much more than that."

After the embarrassment he'd put her through, she sorely wanted to throw a barb and wrench this out-of-control situation back into some kind of order. But another less belligerent part of her wanted to accept his compliment graciously. This situation wasn't ideal...

But it wasn't *all* bad.

She'd *never* been kissed like that before. She was still quaking, every nerve-ending singing as if they'd all been zapped by some heaven-sent force. She wished their embrace hadn't happened in such a public forum; she wasn't certain she would ever live down her flagrant show of abandon in front of so many. But she couldn't deny that the experience had been a huge boost to her confidence. The heat Pace conjured in her *couldn't* be drawn from an ice queen, and instinct said he was capable of stoking that fire a whole lot higher.

So, hoping that her eyes were indeed sparkling, she simply smiled. He returned a dazzling smile of his own, but when he headed for the automatic glass doors—without thinking to put her down—a prickle of panic caught at the back of her throat.

"What are you doing?" The door came nearer and she pushed against his chest—for all the good it did. His stride didn't miss a beat. "Where are you taking me?"

She'd kissed him back. Yes, had revelled in it. But she hadn't waved a limit-free green flag. He knew kidnapping was illegal, right?

"I believe I mentioned a favour," he said, still walking, and her thoughts wound back.

Yes, he *had* mentioned something about returning the favour of taking the time to deliver her car personally. She'd thought he'd meant to toy with her again and convince her to put her hands somewhere on his body. She'd ended up doing that, and more, all on her own.

Her throat closed as the exit drew nearer. A gleaming black sports car sat parked on the building's forecourt, its spokes shining and its lines straight out of a Bond film. *This* was her Brodricks loaner? She could envisage Pace slipping her into the passenger side, him sliding behind the wheel and stealing her away to heaven knew where to do heaven knew what.

She let out a trembling sigh.

How certain was she that she wanted to protest?

Her toes curled as she asked, "Exactly how big is this favour?"

"Let's just say…" he flicked her a glance and winked "…it won't hurt."

She swallowed.

Well, that was good to know.

"Whatever it is," she said, "I can walk. You can put me down."

"I could. But I'm having too much fun."

Flattered, and taken aback, she gaped at him. "You don't give up, do you?"

"Not when I know I'm right. Tell me you didn't enjoy our kiss."

She crossed her arms and looked away. Always fishing. He didn't need her affirmation.

Outside now, Pace pulled up. When he didn't speak or let her down she warily met his gaze. His blue eyes were hooded, but bright in the sunlight—bright and burning with intent. She held her breath as he lifted her higher in his arms and angled his head, pretending he was hard of hearing.

"I'm sorry?" he said. "Did you say something?"

As he spoke, his raspy jaw turned slightly and gently grazed her temple, carefully trailed her cheek. Her body reacted, humming with need, as if her flesh and her blood were programmed to sit up and beg whenever the promise of intimate contact with this man became anything near a possibility.

She wanted to tell him to show a little mercy and give her some breathing space. But, much more, she wanted the delicious sensation he whipped up inside her to go on. Seriously—if he could kiss like that, how would the rest of his repertoire pan out? How would it be to know Pace Davis fully unleashed and acting purely on animal instinct? If *he* couldn't set her fireworks off, no one could. Surely neither of them would be disappointed?

Pace's jaw skimmed her chin, her heart began to thump and her heavy eyes drifted closed. When his lips brushed hers, both nipples fired up beneath her filmy blouse.

He nipped her bottom lip and ran his tongue along the seam. "Say it. Say you want me to kiss you again."

Her stomach muscles quivered, and she moaned in her throat as his mouth lingered agonisingly close.

Phoebe held herself taut, told herself to think of the consequences if things should go bad. But the urge to surrender was greater than the need to take her next breath.

Oh, what the hell?

Her arms looped around his neck and she raised herself to meet his mouth. For better or worse, she was ready to start talking.

CHAPTER FOUR

THE comment came from behind.

"Hang on a minute. I'll go sell some tickets."

Deep into a kiss which was, unbelievably, better than their first, Phoebe snapped her mind back a heartbeat before her eyes sprang open. She was in front of Goldmar Studios, locking lips with a man who could prove to be either her saviour or her ruin.

Now they had company.

Phoebe broke from the embrace and realigned her vision. At the same time her stomach dropped. Steve Trundy looked immaculate, in custom-made trousers, a glorious tan and designer lenses which graced the bridge of his perfectly chiselled nose. When Steve removed his shades, his eyes were filled with scorn.

"If you're quite finished—" her boss began, but then he focused on the other man and his cleft chin was tucked in. "Davis? Is that you?"

"Phoebe invited me to sit in on a recording," Pace replied, as easily as if they'd bumped into each other at the supermarket. "Thought I'd take her up on it."

As Pace settled Phoebe on her feet, Steve arched a speculative brow. "I see you had a good time."

Pace grinned. "Never doubted it."

Steve's lip curled before he tamed his expression. Phoebe could read his thoughts. Wouldn't do to draw swords with the manager of one of the network's biggest sources of advertising dollars. He liked his job too much to upset the accountants.

Instead Steve honed his attention upon Phoebe again. "You didn't return my call yesterday."

Phoebe felt Pace tense beside her, and a hot wave of testosterone rippled out. As usual, Steve's tone was condescending, but Pace didn't need to get involved in her fight. She could look after herself—calmly and with dignity. She didn't want to give Steve any excuse to ball her out any more than he already did.

Playing the unreturned call down, she shrugged. "Sorry. Must have missed it totally."

"We need to talk." Steve slotted his shades into his shirt pocket. "Actually, *you* just need to listen."

Phoebe almost rolled her eyes. It was hard to believe she'd ever thought herself in love with this guy. So full of self-importance. So ready to puff out his chest and bully if he could.

She stood her ground. "I don't have a lot of time right now—"

"I suggest you *make* time," Steve growled.

"Guess you didn't hear." His voice a flinty warning, ready to ignite, Pace took one measured step forward. "The lady said she's in a hurry."

A muscle ticked in Steve's cleanshaven jaw as he evaluated the odds. His opponent was almost a head taller, broader through the shoulders, and he carried an inherent power with the same authority as a royal wore his crown. If Steve started a fight, Pace would finish it.

Steve narrowed assessing eyes, flared his nostrils, but ultimately slid his hands in a conciliatory manner into his chinos' pockets.

"I don't have a beef with you, Davis. I want to speak to my employee."

Pace grinned without humour. "She's clocked off."

Steve's eyes flashed, but then he slowly smiled—a knowing, man-to-man grin. Scratching his temple, he uttered an aside. "I wouldn't waste my time if I were you." He wrinkled his nose, as if to say, *I've been there and she's not worth it.*

While Phoebe's throat closed and her hands fisted by her sides, Pace replied, "Thanks for the tip. Here's one for you." He stepped into the lesser man's space. "If I ever hear you speak like that again, I'll break your jaw."

When Pace opened the Aston Martin's passenger side door Phoebe, apparently still dazed, automatically slid in. A moment later Pace positioned himself behind the wheel and, still fuming, clipped his seatbelt on. That unscheduled meeting with his brother earlier—and chewing it over in the studio all morning—had put him in the right mood to deal with that pompous ass. Any man who insulted a woman needed a crash course on "manners or else". He was almost sorry Trundy hadn't shaped up.

"Sorry about that," Phoebe muttered into her lap. "Steve can be a real jerk sometimes."

"You don't need to apologise." Pace ignited the engine and swerved the vehicle out of the park. "Except maybe to yourself. I'm guessing there's a history between you two that goes beyond nine to five."

None of his business, perhaps, but, dammit, he was bristling and he wanted to know.

Staring blankly out of the window, she gnawed on a thumbnail. "It was a mistake."

Understatement of the year.

"I have a policy." He steered out onto the main drag. "Keep work separate."

"Except in my case?"

He frowned across. "We don't work together."

"We're connected through business."

"Loosely."

She gave him a flat look. "Your company sponsors my show."

"Marketing isn't my department. I was only at that sponsorship event where we met because my br—"

He bit off the word and, acid rising in his gut, cleared his throat. She didn't need to know that much about his background. Frankly, he didn't want to discuss it.

"The president of the company," he amended, "wasn't available." Nick approved advertising budgets, among other things. Pace approved cars. "Besides, you can't put me in the same category as that meathead."

Trundy's insinuation played over in his mind again. It was so off beam Pace couldn't help but grin.

"What's the joke?"

"Trundy," he said, "trying to tell me you're a dud." If Phoebe Moore was frigid, he wore wings and ballet shoes after midnight.

Rubbing her arms and crossing her legs, she slid a wary look over. "What makes you so sure he isn't right?"

Pace grabbed the gearstick and changed down. "Let me pull over and I'll show you."

The way she responded when his mouth covered hers was proof enough. Her surrender was instinctive and, to put it mildly, highly arousing. Phoebe wasn't frigid. She wasn't even hot. She was *scorching*.

Letting him kiss her a second time said that she was finally leaning towards his way of thinking—that they owed it to themselves and each other to take this fierce attraction to the next electrifying level. To leave off finishing what they'd started today would be a crime. He only wished she didn't have somewhere else to be.

But there was always tomorrow. He'd waited this long for the privilege. He could wait a little longer.

Her cellphone rang. As he strangled the wheel, Pace's smile turned into a sneer. He almost hoped it was Trundy. He'd like nothing better than to turn this baby around and show that baboon he hadn't been joking.

Phoebe fished her phone from her bag, answered, then cried out, "Oh, no! Is he okay?" When Pace flicked a concerned look her way, she nodded, sighed, and drove a hand through her hair. "No, I understand, Wendy. I'll organise something else. Sure. Thanks for letting me know."

A yellow light changed to red, and Pace brought the purring Aston to a standstill. Phoebe was staring, unseeing, dead ahead.

"Trouble?" he asked.

"My trip to Tyler's Stream is off."

His brows shot up. So wishes did come true. They could spend the day together. He would have been inordinately pleased if she hadn't looked so down. "What's the problem?"

"I had a handyman lined up this afternoon to finish a job at my aunt's house. That was his wife. Daryl fell while he was cleaning out some roof gutters today. Broke his leg. A compound fracture."

Pace flinched. Nasty. "What job was he doing?"

"Near the end of last winter my aunt's boiler died. Meg thought she could battle through, but she ended up in hospital with pneumonia. She brought Daryl out to see if the boiler could be repaired. He gave her a price and ordered in the part. It's still sitting in the basement."

A bus of Japanese tourists roared across the intersection and the light turned green. "Your aunt's not so good at taking care of those things?" he surmised, and she nodded. "So today you were making sure the job was done before winter kicked in?"

She nodded again. "Meg's due back from overseas in just over a month. I won't sit back and take a chance on her landing back in hospital." She concentrated on her phone. "I'll just have to organise someone else for next weekend."

"I could fit the part."

She sent over a small smile. "Thanks, but it's a radiator, not a V8 engine."

"To us mechanics, it's much of a muchness."

She sat straighter and thought for a moment. "I couldn't ask you to do that."

But the sparkle in her eyes told him she wanted to. She obviously cared for this aunt a great deal. Sure, he wanted time with her—wanted the opportunity to kiss her again—but he also wanted to help.

"You didn't ask," he pointed out. "I offered."

"It's a long drive."

He shifted up a gear and joined the streams of traffic filing over the Harbour Bridge. "I like long drives."

"My dog might be put out. He's not used to sharing me."

"I'll only bite if he does."

Phoebe succumbed to a smile, then buried it quick. "I'll accept—but on one condition."

If the condition was not kissing her again, he wouldn't agree the terms. "Shoot."

Her beautiful mouth lifted into a challenging grin. "At some stage I get to sit behind that wheel."

A woman after his own heart.

He laughed and stepped on the gas. "It's a deal."

Phoebe clicked open her apartment door, explaining, "My dog isn't used to company. He can be a little difficult if he doesn't know you."

"Don't worry," Pace assured her. "I grew up with dogs. Man's best friend and all that."

She sent a look that said he just didn't get it, then fanned open the door.

The puppy on the couch sat up, pixie ears pricked. On seeing his mistress, he dropped his ears and his tail thumped like a piston against the cushions. Then he saw Pace. The tail stopped dead. A rumbling growl gathered, then snapped like a midget clap of thunder across the room.

"Hannie!" Phoebe barked back. "Behave yourself."

The pup—Hannie—fell onto his stomach, setting his snout on his outstretched front paws. Pace shifted his jaw. Poor little guy was only protecting his mistress. He got that. He'd bet the dog and Trundy hadn't got on so well.

"I won't be a minute," Phoebe said, heading for a

doorway that led, Pace presumed, to her bedroom. "I'll change and pack a few things."

"Fine," he called back. "Hannie and I'll get acquainted."

Pace flung over a genial salute, one boy buddy to another. The pint-sized dog cocked his head and his rhinestone collar sparkled.

"What say you and I get any concerns out in the open?" Pace said, sauntering over. "Then we can concentrate on enjoying a pleasant afternoon together, just the three of us. What do you say?" Pace made himself comfortable on the couch, angled towards the mutt, and stretched out a hand. "Friends?"

Inches from Pace's fingers, ferocious tiny teeth snapped, then clattered like a rapid spurt of gunfire. Heartbeat hammering, Pace scrambled sideways off the couch.

"What's going on out there?"

Pace ignored Phoebe's call from the bedroom long enough to count his fingers. He blew on each digit then, shuddering, shook out his shoulders and arms. "Uh, just me and Hannie making friends."

Setting his jaw, recalibrating his perceptions, Pace squared off in front of the mutt. Hannie bared those ninja teeth, his top lip drawn back to his nose. Pace exercised his neck, rotated his shoulders.

Then found a cynical grin.

This scene didn't feel a whole lot different from the face-off he'd had with Nick this morning. One of so many.

Growing up, Pace had heard over and again how much the brothers resembled one another. In looks and habits, perhaps, but their brains were chalk and cheese.

Nick was a figures man through and through, while Pace lived for adrenaline rushes—particularly getting behind the wheel of a hot car. That mutual love of and fascination with automobiles was the reason his father had left *him* in charge of the company.

Nicholas Senior had shaped his younger son for the role from his early teens. Part of Pace had basked in the attention, and in his father's belief in his abilities. Nicholas Senior had been a powerful character. Everyone had wanted to please him.

But another well-hidden part of the younger Brodrick boy had almost resented being groomed for a job which, deep down, he'd felt only half equipped to handle. A job he'd known he could never do as well as his financially brilliant dad. Every time he saw Nick now, and they invariably butted heads, Pace was reminded of the thumping magnitude with which that prediction had come true.

From as far back as dot he and Nick had been in competition…on the tennis court, for high school girls, but particularly for their father's attention and approval. Pace didn't want to dwell on who their father's favourite would be now if he were alive, but his half-brother never tired of finding subtle ways to stick it in. Point in case this morning.

In to collect the Aston for Phoebe, he'd found Nick basking behind his desk. His brother had asked again about those figures he needed on Monday; he didn't want any mistakes and had suggested Pace double-check to make sure they were right. Triple-check if need be.

His temper had boiled. Like so many other times in his life, Pace had wanted to slog him.

A knock echoed through the living room, and Pace swung towards the door at the same time as Phoebe emerged from the bedroom, her hair a sheet of silk and her angelic curves breathtaking beneath a flowing white dress. Pace's skin heated as a groan of brewing desire replaced the pent-up angst of a moment ago. When her jewelled eyes flashed an easy smile as she passed, Pace's blood simmered more. He couldn't wait to see how the rest of their day panned out—even with the mutt along.

Phoebe opened the door to an elderly lady and exclaimed, "Oh, good morning, Mrs G!"

Setting his private thoughts aside, Pace nodded politely towards a woman wearing a jet-black rinse and a multi-coloured shift. As "Mrs G" entered the room, she regarded the two thoughtfully, worrying her jaw back and forth as if ill-fitting dentures were terrorising her gums.

"Didn't mean to interrupt anything," she said. A single bark sounded as Hannie leapt over into the older woman's arms, and those assessing eyes suddenly glistened with unabashed love. "How are you, darling boy?"

Pace swallowed uncomfortably as kisses—the wet kind, involving at least two mouths and one tongue—were exchanged.

"You're not interrupting, Mrs G," Phoebe said, guiding her visitor into the room.

"I wanted to know if you needed me this weekend."

"Actually," Phoebe said, "we're about to head off for the country."

The woman's expression sharpened. "To your aunt's

place? Be nice this time of year." She eyed Pace like a headmistress summing up a possible truant.

Phoebe gestured to Pace. "This is a friend of mine—Pace Davis."

The old biddy glared. "You like dogs, Mr Davis?"

"Sure," he answered jauntily. "*Hot*—with mustard and pickles." He chuckled, but fell silent when everyone, including the hairball, simply stared. He tugged his ear. *Bad joke.*

After sizing him up a final time, Mrs G turned to Phoebe. "I wanted to let you know that I have an appointment next Wednesday. Not till late."

Phoebe turned to usher the older woman out. "I'll make sure I'm home early to take Hannie off your hands if he's over there."

Mrs G dropped a kiss on the dog's crown. "You be a good boy. No chasing possums, hmm?" She looked down her nose at Pace. "No need to tell *you* to behave, I hope?"

Pace smiled ear to ear. "I haven't chased a possum in years."

"Goodbye, Mrs G." Taking Hannie, Phoebe politely showed the frowning woman to the door. When Mrs G was out of earshot, Phoebe shrugged apologetically. "She's really very sweet when you get to know her."

Pace shuddered. "A veritable bee at the hive."

Phoebe gave his arm a playful slap as she wove around and headed for the kitchen. "I'll pack some provisions," she called over a shoulder.

Sensing an outing, Hannie scampered across the timber floor to camp out by the front door. Pace surrendered to a grin. Smart dog. A little *too* smart.

Pace cast an eye around the apartment. A couple

of surrealist paintings on the wall, air-con installed. Comfortable furniture strewn with bright cushions.

He spotted a loose sheet of paper on the side-table and scooped it up.

"'Phoebe's Wish List'," he muttered aloud, then shook his head, smiling. Typical organised female. Making a list for Christmas already.

His eye ran down the page before his vision scudded back to the top. A hot bath of hope poured over him as he reread that very inviting first point: *Find Mr Right Now.*

Impressed, Pace let out a low whistle. He wondered how many requests Santa got for *that*.

He peered around the corner. With Phoebe still busy in the kitchen, his attention went back to the list.

Guess it wasn't such a strange request. It was the twenty-first century, after all. Today's women were supposed to be into careers and having it all. Being tied down to a Mr Right with a couple of kids made that difficult. Hell, he was about to turn thirty and he was nowhere near ready for that kind of commitment. Playing the field was a good alternative—it seemed for both sexes.

But if having a memorable affair was at the top of Phoebe's wish list, there were only two explanations for her hard-to-get act these past weeks. It was either simply that—a tantalising act, as he'd always suspected—or she hadn't considered him a contender for the position.

Those couple of kisses today ought to leave her in no doubt.

Either way, it seemed as if it was Tyler's Stream and smooth sailing from here on.

CHAPTER FIVE

HER aunt's boiler was going to be fixed. Hannie hadn't yet tried to eat her handsome companion's face. She and Pace were enjoying each other's company, even outside of their usual flirting mode. Despite its unconventional beginning, today was turning out to be a good one.

Halfway to Tyler's Stream, however, Phoebe's buoyant mood dipped.

As they motored down a lonely stretch of highway in a high-powered British car that diamond-studded dreams were made of, Phoebe noticed the windscreen had begun to spot with rain. The day had begun with a flawless blue sky, but as they'd headed south rain clouds had crept in. She checked the rearview mirror.

No cars behind them. Nothing up ahead. Nevertheless, she slowed down ten Ks.

"Ready for me to take over, or do you plan to hog the wheel the whole way?" Sitting relaxed beside her, Pace chose another CD from the stash Phoebe had brought along.

These past two hours they'd listened to music while Hannie had napped in the back on the sumptuous leather seat. They'd discussed holidays and movies, but thankfully he hadn't mentioned this morning's incidents—either those crazy-mad kisses they'd shared or the Steve Trundy debacle. Perhaps Pace didn't want her attention distracted too much while she sat in charge of a machine that would dent a bank balance at least two hundred grand. He must have a stack of clout at Brodricks to have organised such an impressive loaner. This car was amazingly smooth, incredibly powerful, and equipped with all the latest gadgets and trimmings. But after two hours she wouldn't mind a swap.

Driving in the rain wasn't her favourite thing.

Exercising her neck, she glanced over. "Think I'll pull up at the next gas station."

The words weren't out before she spotted a huge blurry mass, the colour of red soil, bounding across the road up ahead. Her heart flew to her throat a second before instinct took over and she slammed on the brakes.

The kangaroo was a monster. If they hit, God knew how much damage would be done—to the car as well as to its passengers. She doubted the kangaroo would survive either.

She heard Pace's expletive as they both held on and the car jerked rapidly, repeatedly, decelerating ultra fast on premium anti-skid brakes. All would have been good if the kangaroo had kept on bouncing its way back into the bush. Instead, powerful hind legs brought it to a thumping stop. As its eyes meshed with hers through the windscreen, Phoebe went cold all over.

They were going to hit.

She wrenched the wheel and the car spun out.

It all happened so fast, and yet in another dimension the scene played out in agonising slow motion. She clutched the wheel, her eyes terrifyingly wide, as the front swept around in a dizzy one-eighty. Like a rag doll, she swung one way and then, with a bruising jolt, the other. As if she were stuck in a nightmare about to get worse, she couldn't find a voice to scream.

When the car finally slammed to a dead stop Phoebe's knuckles were white, her legs were newborn-foal-weak, and the Aston Martin was facing north instead of south.

Unable to move, even to blink, she sat, dazed, trying to get her mind around what had just happened while her heart hammered high in her throat. When the driver's side door was flung open she gasped and shot a look up.

Pace was frowning at her, a vein pulsing erratically down one side of his brow.

"Move over," he ordered. "We need to get off the road before a semi or a family in a sedan come up over that hill."

Feeling as if she were standing on a slanting deck in the middle of a storm, she threw a glance at the empty seat beside her. When he nudged her arm, forcing her mind and shaky limbs into action, she shuffled over the gearstick. Pace leapt in and, with precision movements, swung the car around and parked it on the road's shoulder.

He flung an arm over the back of the passenger headrest. His face was as dark as hers felt pale. When his warm firm palm cupped the back of her head and he urged her head gently more towards him her chest exploded with a tempest of emotion.

Relief. Infinite gratitude. They hadn't hit. They weren't injured, or worse. She wanted to throw her arms around his neck and never let go.

His concentrated gaze swept over her, top to toe. "Are you all right?"

Her body had been invaded by the shakes. Her hands trembled uncontrollably, and if she tried to speak her teeth might very well chatter. She'd never been in a car accident before, but her mother had. The worst kind.

The worst outcome.

Her lungs begging for air, Phoebe sucked in a breath, but she couldn't catch the tear trailing down her cheek. Pace leaned over and, holding her close, rubbed her back.

"It's okay," he murmured against her ear, stroking her hair as a growling truck hurtled past and the car vibrated. "You're okay now."

She focused her every fibre on his warmth and his strength. She felt Tyler's Stream so close now. The memories...good and bad. She'd grown up in a nice home, with plenty to eat and plenty of love.

Yes, she *was* okay. More than okay.

But what would have become of her without Aunt Meg?

An hour later Pace steered the Aston Martin up a pair of shallow ruts that led to a remote, quaint-looking house in the small town of Tyler's Stream...the place Phoebe had at one time called home. The clouds had dispersed again, and a tranquil sun was arcing towards the west.

She'd remained quiet the rest of the journey here. Pace had been rather subdued too.

That spinout would have tamped down anyone's mood, but the car hadn't been damaged and no one had been hurt—thank God. She'd never forget the harrowing feeling when she'd thought they were seconds from colliding with that gigantic roo. It was as if every iota of energy had been sucked from her heart down her legs and out through her toes. Neither would she forget how Pace had held and comforted her afterwards.

She'd been too shaken to feel silly or weak. She'd accepted his reassurance gladly, and was grateful he hadn't let her go until he'd known she was ready. It was odd to think of the turns their relationship had taken since five p.m. yesterday afternoon. She'd seen another side to her heart-throb bad boy and she liked it. A lot.

For the past hour Hannie had enjoyed the cool rush of wind on his face from the back seat. There hadn't been one peep out of him the entire time—even after the incident. But now the engine was barely cut before her little dog jumped out, yapping as he raced to the cottage's front door. Once there, he sat still as any statue, waiting for his mistress to unlock it and let him in.

Chuckling, Pace opened the passenger door. "Does he usually get so wound up about his visits to the country?"

"Sure," Phoebe replied, slipping out of the passenger side. "It's nice…to visit."

Moving forward, Phoebe took in the scene, and an odd, hazy sense of the past returned. The place looked the same. *Felt* the same. A haven as well as a sentence. Pristine lace curtains hung neatly in every window. The front door was lacquered that same deep red. The walls might have been whitewashed only yesterday.

Either side of the flagstone path pink and violet wildflowers were fading on the dragging heels of summer. The lawn, however, was its usual clumpy green self. The sky was again flawless, of a hue and depth postcards from exotic lands could only hope to fudge. And the air was fresh and strangely heady; not a factory stack or congested freeway for miles. Subtle smells—damp black soil, eucalypt mixed with minty pine—reminded her of long talks, shared laughter, and sometimes tears.

From the boot, Pace found the hamper, and the toolbox which they'd collected from Brodricks on the way through. When Phoebe swung open the front door Hannie shot forward, hurling himself up onto his favourite spot—beneath the framed autographed poster of Jimi Hendrix that hung one side of a stone fireplace.

Pace set down the hamper, then made his way to the centre of the room, his gaze skating over the surrounds: a meditative pyramid frame in one corner, crystals hanging from doorways, a mound of LPs stashed against the wall company for the polished radiogram…

"This is…" He nodded, poker-faced. "Well, it's *weird*." Phoebe laughed, and his expression broke into a relieved grin that said he was glad she understood. "I feel like I've stepped into a time warp." A psychedelic print on the far wall must have leapt out at him, because he rubbed his eyes as if they hurt.

Phoebe swept a fanfare gesture through the air. "Welcome to Tyler's Stream's shrine to the sixties."

"Good ol' sex, drugs and rock 'n' roll?"

"Meg would be more comfortable with *peace*, love and rock 'n' roll." Phoebe tipped her head at an Elvis wall clock, the hips of which swivelled back and forth with every tick. "*Lots* of rock 'n' roll."

Strolling by a credenza, Pace ran a finger along the

frame of what Phoebe knew was her aunt's pride and joy…a photo of Meg, resplendent in flower-power gear, lying on a peace sign at Woodstock with her "pal", Janis Joplin. His initial expression of scepticism disappeared when Pace raised the frame to scrutinise it further. He cocked a brow.

"Your Aunt Meg gets around."

"Let's say she has a way with people. You couldn't guess at some of her acquaintances these days."

He slid another appreciative glance around. "Bet this would've been one crazy place to hang out on vacations."

Phoebe crossed to remove the rocking chair's dust-sheet. "My friends thought it was pretty cool. Weird, but cool." Then she digested what he'd said. "Vacations? No. I grew up here." His brow knitted, questioning. Of course—he wouldn't know. "Just me and my aunt after my mother died. I was four."

Pace's expression disintegrated. "Oh, Phoebe… God, I'm sorry." Blindly he replaced the photo. "You don't have any brothers or sisters?"

Winding the dustsheet over her arms, Phoebe shook her head. That was definitely a downer. She would have loved a younger sister to pamper and protect. Someone to share things with…jokes, clothes, memories. She envied people who had that.

"What about your dad?" he asked.

The crystals tinkled in a disturbed air current as she hurled the sheet at a corner in order to delay her answer. Dads were not her choice subject.

"I don't have a father."

He studied her for a long moment. "You mean you didn't know him?" he said quietly.

At the dining room window, she drew back the cream lace to unlatch it.

"Is there a difference? When you're a child," she explained slowly, "never knowing a person and that person never existing amounts to pretty much the same thing."

When she'd visited friends' houses, watched their parents together, or listened when their fathers spoke about respecting their elders or such stuff, she'd wondered what it would be like to have a daddy all her own. She'd felt…different. Often on the outside looking in. By junior school she realised some people thought of her in that light, too. Being born illegitimate was considered by many to be a sin—at least in her small hometown.

By college, it had all become too hard.

Those memories stirred up too many bad feelings. She'd sooner push them aside and concentrate on the now.

She turned and saw that the sympathy she'd heard in Pace's voice was mirrored in his face. But she wanted the vibrant blue in his eyes to sparkle again. She didn't want to dwell on the past.

"The boiler's down here," she announced breezily, determined to set the tone back on track. She strode toward an alcove that led to the basement and fanned open its door. "How long do you think it'll take?"

Toolbox in hand, he brushed by. One powerful arm whispering against hers was enough to make her quiver and remember how his lips had felt against hers—skilled and instantly drugging.

But she was still a little shaken from the accident. For now she'd focus on the job at hand.

Willing away the pleasant twinge low in her belly, she flicked a switch, igniting two naked lightbulbs hanging from their straggly cords.

Pace headed down. "I'll let you know when I'm finished. Might take five minutes." He disappeared down the well. "Or half the night."

Thirty minutes later, Pace spun a final watertight wrench on the remaining bolt and stood back to evaluate his work. The part for the boiler had fitted with no problem. Hopefully dear Aunt Meg's winters would be snug for a long time to come.

He packed his gear, knowing this basement saw the light of those bulbs rarely. Rows of mouldy-smelling boxes lined numerous shelves. Neat piles of musty books lay stacked in a corner. Auntie collected artefacts: a pair of six-foot regal-looking giraffes; one ginormous smiling Buddha; too-many-to-count rolls of what he guessed were tapestries. Everything had its place.

Pace ascended the creaky steps, thinking how alike he and Meg were. He, too, liked to have things where they ought to be. From a lad, every spanner had been routinely put away. At university every line and dimension on his engineering drawings had been exact. Always calibrations were checked to the nth degree.

Nick was the same with following the stock market and analysing loopholes to keep money shifting to make the most of every tax break and investment opportunity. Yes, he and Nick were similar, too.

And so damn different.

He edged out into the bright light of the Moores' living room. He'd declined Phoebe's offer of refreshment when she'd visited the basement earlier. Now, however, he was parched. And starved. He hadn't eaten since breakfast, and his growling stomach was reminding him every two minutes.

Finding the kitchen, he took a casual inventory. Autographed memorabilia from twentieth-century legends didn't line these counters. Just rows of tan tiles bordering a scarred hardwood bench, a menagerie of utensils hanging over an old woodstove.

He checked out the next room from a distance.

No Phoebe.

He was about to move on when his gaze hooked on a pair of photos perched on the window ledge—six-by-fours set in a tarnished silver double frame. On one side a happy and beautiful young woman—bearing a striking resemblance to Phoebe—held a tiny baby up for the camera. No mistaking the identical river of pale blond hair streaked with gold, the sparkling green eyes.

On the alternate side beamed an unusually pretty girl with a familiar heart-shaped face…Phoebe, aged perhaps nine or ten, curled around a tyre-swing hanging from some big old tree. Something small clutched in her hand—a penknife?—had caught a glint of sun. Her smile was so total the upward thrust of her cheeks left only happy slits for eyes.

Pace's heart pinched.

So this was the little girl who had grown up without her parents.

He dragged a finger across the glass. The dust-free line left Phoebe's smile brighter still.

Pace's father had been an exceedingly busy and enterprising man, and an exacting, larger-than-life person as well as a mentor to whom Pace could never hope to measure up. But at a pinch Nicholas Senior had made himself available if either boy had ever truly needed him—even if gaining his undivided attention had taken some doing. The positive as well as the negative... Pace couldn't imagine growing up without his father's influence.

Then there was Phoebe, who'd not only missed out on a father but on a mother's guidance too. She'd had her aunt. But still...

He studied the photos and his bite clenched.

What man could walk away from his own flesh and blood?

Phoebe pushed on the cottage's back door and, seeing the silhouette of a tall broad figure standing in Meg's kitchen, reflexively reeled back. She wasn't used to seeing a man in this house—*any* man. But, sucking down a breath, she soon realised.

Holding her clamouring heart, she exhaled heavily.

"Pace, you scared me half to death."

He looked a little taken aback himself, setting the photo frames he'd been holding back on the counter.

"I've finished the boiler," he said, stepping forward. "Thought I'd find out where everyone was hiding."

"I was out back."

"Out back where?" Pace craned his neck to peer around her.

Hooking an arm, Phoebe retraced her steps through the doorway and Pace followed.

Scattered gums and clusters of firs stretched to distant purple hills. Untouched, unhurried smells wove all around…old wood, scented wildflowers, and the purest of fresh country air. It was *beautiful*. And yet Phoebe hadn't been able to leave this town behind her quickly enough. Her aunt aside, home was supposed to be where the heart was—but if her heart lay in Tyler's Stream she'd have to dig deep to find it.

"When I hit seventeen Meg and I renovated the old housemaid's quarters," she told him, letting them both inside a smaller cottage that lay at the end of the path. "It was great, having my own space filled with my own things, listening to my own music whenever I liked. But I had responsibilities, too. Cleaning, cooking, setting my own bedtime."

She'd felt so grown up. But she had never over-stepped the boundaries. Never dreamed of inviting boys back in the middle of the night. She wouldn't have betrayed Meg's trust that way. More importantly, she hadn't wanted to end up like her mother…starry-eyed, in love, then pregnant and alone. A child deserved two parents. Hell, *she'd* deserved at least one.

As they moved further inside—the lower level a living space, an open attic the bedroom—Pace nodded his approval.

"Cosy." He took in the *faux* bearskin rug stretched between the fireplace and an Indian cotton couch. The far wall was painted cerise. When his survey hit the counter, his eyes flashed.

"Ah! There you are."

Phoebe glanced over and smiled. He was talking to the hamper.

"Guess you're ready now?"

She'd meant for coffee, but she didn't miss the spark in his gaze at her suggestion—or the sizzling undercurrent that zapped a lightning path from his eyes straight to hers.

Instantly light-headed, she angled back to boil the water.

She'd seen that look in his eye before. A look that said he wanted what he wanted, and right now he wanted her. Earlier today, back in Sydney, she'd thought she'd wanted him too. Now, after their near accident, in this setting…

Well, she felt more cautious. Edgy.

Holding her stomach, she flicked on the kettle. "Coffee or cocoa?" she asked a little absently.

When he didn't answer, she looked back over her shoulder.

As if it were a difficult choice, Pace had tilted his head. He moved towards her, nearer and nearer, until his mouth eventually stopped a breath away from hers. The dark bristles on his jaw glistened in the silver threads of light slanting in through the window.

Then that masculine mouth grinned and suddenly, like an urge to jump, Phoebe's fingertips burned to sample the sandpaper-roughness of those cheeks and compare the abrasion to those soft smiling lips. She still felt edgy, but where Pace was concerned she couldn't seem to keep the longing she felt for him down.

He said, "I think I like the sound of cocoa." His deep voice resonated through her blood like chords of music before he lobbed an unhurried glance over his shoulder to the fireplace, the couch. "It's almost cold enough for a fire," he said, as his eyes climbed the ladder and then swam back to focus once more upon her lips. A lopsided smile hooked his mouth, perfectly aligned teeth appearing as his smile grew. "Shall we drive it in?"

Quivering inside, Phoebe swallowed hard.

She knew his mind: cocoa first, soft mattress and crisp sheets later. After the explosion of those kisses earlier she really couldn't blame him.

Low and deep inside, that giddy spiral of longing intensified, the heart-thumping sensation spreading over her body like a delicious rash. Nape, nipples, fingertips—everything tingled. Despite her past experiences…the doubts she harboured about herself… wouldn't sleeping with Pace Davis be the easiest, most natural thing in the world?

His lidded eyes held hers. "I have an idea. But we'll need a few things."

Phoebe's heartbeat skipped. A few things like, maybe, massage oil? Body chocolate?

"Do you have a Thermos?"

Phoebe blinked. Did he say… "A *Thermos*?"

"And a blanket? The picnic kind."

She blinked again. "Yes, I have a blanket…and a Thermos."

"It'll be dark soon." Moving to a window, Pace drew back the curtain to inspect a horizon hinting at the rose-hewn colours of sunset. "We'll take the cocoa with us on a walk. And didn't you say there was apple pie?"

Phoebe risked a peek at the loft, visualised two bodies wreathing and on the brink, then she saw it as it actually was—a quaint room with a neat quilted bed, shelves chock-full of memories, a box filled with her childhood dress-ups, and a one-eyed teddy bear propped on his cushions. A young woman's retreat from her small-minded world.

Still, as they put pie and drinks together for their picnic, his scent filled her lungs, his heat teased her skin, and Phoebe couldn't help but wonder if it was time for her loft to grow up, too.

CHAPTER SIX

TEN minutes later they were strolling beside a pretty winding stream that reminded Pace of the countryside when he'd visited Germany—verdant green and breathtakingly picturesque. The last of the sun was hanging onto the day as a cool breeze drifted in from the silhouetted hills. Hannie had trotted off ahead, trusting Pace with his mistress as he disappeared into the grass.

Pace inhaled a lung full of fresh air. "Ever miss these wide open spaces?"

"Sometimes. Meg and my mother loved the country. That house was their parents', and their parents' before them. Meg used to reminisce for hours about their 'adventures in the wilderness' when they were young."

"Sounds like they were good mates," Pace said, thinking about Nick and how they'd never seen eye to eye but rather *had* constantly competed. Growing up, it had always been who hit the ball hardest? Or whose mud pies were the biggest? Between his father's expectations and his brother's goading Pace had been constantly kept on his toes. But he'd more than held his own. Until that one god-awful, very public disgrace. Now he only had to *look* at his brother to be reminded of how badly he'd stuffed up three years ago. It aggravated the bejesus out of him.

And Nick knew it.

"Meg was a little older," Phoebe was saying, "and a lot wiser. When my mother fell for a man passing through, Meg was there to comfort her."

She stooped to pluck a flower while Pace put two and two together. The man had been Phoebe's father.

"Ever try to find him?" he asked.

Twirling the stem, Phoebe gazed off at some distant point and lifted her chin. "Other people might want to track down their biological links. I don't need to go there."

Pace thought he understood. "Guess it wouldn't change anything."

"I'm over wondering about what happened to him. But there are some things I'd change if I could."

"Like?"

"Like my mother never giving up on the idea that one day he'd come back to her. She was driving to see him the night she died. It was a wet night. A tired truck driver nodded off and…" She tossed the flower away. "Well, she never came back."

Pace's stomach fell. Her mother had died in a car accident? She'd had reason enough to be shaken earlier, when their car had spun out. Having lost her mother that way must have made that near miss all the more harrowing.

The line between her brows eased. "But I had my aunt. She loved me like a daughter, and I've always looked on her as a parent. I don't know what I'd have done without Meg." Her mouth tightened almost imperceptibly. "Sometimes I wish I could tell my mother that."

Pace had to swallow to dislodge the stone in his throat. Not only had she been dumped by her father, Phoebe also felt abandoned by her mother—a woman who had been responsible for a small child but had driven off on a wet night to visit an ex who'd no longer wanted her.

His own father might have worked too hard, but Pace knew he'd slogged those long hours not only for his own sense of satisfaction but also for his family's sake, for their security. Pace's grandfather had been an alcoholic who'd squandered the family budget on booze and terrorised the home at night in drunken rages. Nicholas Senior had wanted different things for his children. That was why he'd put in those hours. Expected so much.

One day he hoped Phoebe could forgive her mother. Carrying around a truck full of spite for someone you ought to love was heavy work. He should know.

Setting the hamper down, he gave a soft smile. "Let's have that cocoa and pie."

She glanced around and nodded. "The perfect spot."

They stood beneath a massive dome of lime-green foliage supported by a giant trunk and a tangle of exposed roots. This monster must stand fifty feet high. A hundred to one it was the swing-tree from that photo in the kitchen he'd looked at.

He laid out the blanket. "What kind of tree is this?" He'd never seen one like it.

"No idea." Kneeling, she extracted the Thermos and cups from the hamper. "Definitely not a pine. Obviously not a gum. In spring its branches are covered with these amazing fluffy white flowers."

Scooping her legs at an angle beneath her, Phoebe poured two steaming cups, then handed one to Pace as he hunkered down beside her.

"Years ago I'd tell myself this tree was magic. That it had grown here on this very spot, overlooking this part of the stream, just for me. Every year, when the blossoms were full enough, the wind strong enough..."

Pace could imagine. "There'd be a massive white carpet?"

"And a snowstorm of flowers floating all around. I'd close my eyes...and dream."

Her eyes drifted shut as an angelic smile lifted the corners of her full-lipped mouth.

Pace's mesmerised gaze swept over her. "What would you dream of?"

A faint vee formed between her brows before she opened her eyes and smiled cryptically. "The usual things little girls dream of."

Close by, Hannie snapped out a clatter of sharp and rapid yaps before streaking off again into the distant wood.

"Rabbits," Phoebe explained. "They drive him nuts—not that he catches any. When he's had enough, he knows his way home." She took a sip, watching him over the rim of her cup. "What about you? Do your parents live in Sydney?"

Pace lowered his cup. "My mother died when I was twelve," he said. "My father when I was twenty-five. A heart attack. My brother and his fiancée live in Sydney."

"I'm sorry about your parents," she murmured, her

voice full of understanding. Then she angled her head. "You always seemed like such a mystery to me."

"Maybe because you were so busy running the other way."

"I'm not running now."

She held his gaze with hers and the air simmered between them. Drawn to her like never before, Pace was about to lean closer when she dropped her eyes and rummaged through the hamper.

The pie was delicious, sweet and filling. The cocoa too. But the air was cooling by degrees now. Pace thought they ought to head back to her cottage soon. Light a fire. Maybe stay the night. And, remarkably, his reasoning wasn't about sex. Not entirely.

He could do the drive back to Sydney, certainly. He'd thought she'd want him to. But after learning about her mother and how she'd died, taking a break from the road until morning might be best.

When he'd finished eating, Pace put his plate in the hamper. Phoebe leaned in at the same time. Their hands brushed and, like a lightning flash, the chemistry that drew them together and fought to hold them there flared up again. Feeling the jolt, too, Phoebe darted her gaze to his.

But his eyes had drifted to her mouth, to the succulent pink bow and the lone pastry crumb that sat, enticing him, on her lower lip.

He didn't think. Didn't hesitate. Acting on instinct, he simply leaned in, cupped her head, and plucked that crumb from her lips with his own.

A shiver of anticipation whirled through Phoebe's centre as Pace's mouth touched hers. A knot of hot need swelled in her throat when, feather-light, their lips touched again, this time lingering. Her eyes drifted shut and a firestorm swept over her skin at the same time as bands of heat coiled and tightened around her core. When a tiny blissful sigh escaped her throat his arm went around her to draw her wonderfully close.

Like a length of warm wax her body moulded to his as a crooked finger tilted her chin higher, angling her face so that his mouth hovered a heady whisper away from hers. Testing, he gently rimmed her lips with the tip of his tongue—first one way, then the other. Disbelieving that an act so simple, so mild, could wind her up so tight, Phoebe gave in to the burn—gave in to it all—and wove her arms around his strong neck.

He kissed her deeply. Thoroughly. Her entire being seemed to shut down before an explosion detonated deep inside and her heart swelled under a rapid rush of blood. She felt exhilarated. Alive. As if she'd sprinted up ten flights of stairs with weights on her belt and angel's wings on her feet. She savoured the flavour of apple and creamy chocolate.

How would the rest of him taste?

His hand slid from the back of her neck down her spine, until his thumb found and rubbed that low, sensitive dip. Swept further away, she cupped his jaw and pressed her sensitive breasts against his chest. As the kiss deepened more he eased her back and onto the blanket, tangled in each other's limbs. His hand trailed down the outside of her smooth leg, then back up, towing material along in its wake.

Her fingers flexed through his hair, urging him closer as she arched up. Blistering magic raced through her veins. There'd never been a sensation like it—brilliant tingling waves of hundred-proof pleasure sparking to hot pulsing life.

The iron of his hand scorched a path over her waist, settling on her hip, kneading till his fingers worked their way beneath her dress.

A low, sure voice hummed at her ear. "I knew you'd feel like this…soft and hot and heavenly." His velvet tongue tickled a lobe. "I want you, Phoebe…I want you more than ever."

Phoebe trembled out a sigh. Oh, Lord, she wanted him too. She'd been consumed by a fire that could never get enough of his fuel. Never enough of his heat and this hunger. When he tasted the hollow at her throat an almost painful longing flooded her. Breathless, she dragged his mouth back up to hers, and as he devoured her again she reached around, prying the shirt from his belt and up over that wide, muscular back.

Feeling reckless, yet in control, she flipped over until he lay on his back and she lay squarely on top, her thighs pressed over his hips. But when she tossed back the hair hanging in her eyes her gaze caught on a spot a few feet away. On her tree…on its trunk…the etching she'd left there so long ago.

In a blinding flash she remembered the day she'd carved that heart and the many times she'd touched it those first few years. She thought of her shiny pen-knife, then of her faded childhood, and how once she'd dreamed of finding not *Mr Right Now* but *Prince Charming*—a dedicated family man who would protect her and always be there for her, the way her mother and father had not.

That was so long ago, but her chest still squeezed thinking of it now, and as a wind from the south blew over her back a familiar frosty cold soaked into her heart. Her stomach muscles gripped, and much of the beautiful warmth Pace had brought out in her was in an instant lost.

Biting her lip, she rolled away.

"I'm sorry," she murmured, avoiding his gaze. "I can't do this."

At least not here. Not in this town. Not near this tree.

Pace pushed up onto his elbows. "What's wrong?"

Heat was returning—not to her blood but to her cheeks. He would never understand. She should never have brought him here. Now she wished she'd never come back. If it weren't for Meg, she wouldn't have.

His warm hand covered hers. "Phoebe?"

She drove out a breath and, feeling empty, looked around. "It's this place."

"I thought you liked this spot."

"I do. I *did*."

He coughed out a laugh. "I'm confused."

Her throat thick, she held her brow, then pushed up to her feet. Of course he was confused. She was being a yo-yo. Whether he understood or not, she owed him an explanation.

"In a small town," she began, "scandals die hard, and some folk believe apples don't fall far from the tree." When he cocked his head, she made it more clear. "There were people waiting for me to turn out like my mother—to fall pregnant, unmarried, then throw my life away chasing rainbows I'd never catch. The kids I went to school with were fine," she said, "but some parents didn't want their girls mixing with my kind."

Illegitimate.

She'd been determined to somehow change the perception people had of her. Change the label she'd inherited but hadn't earned. At fourteen, when her girlfriends had been watching their weight and experimenting with hair dye and boys, she'd chopped her hair short and hid her developing figure in overalls. Just to prove it to Tyler's Stream, she hadn't so much as kissed a boy until she'd moved away.

She crossed to the tree trunk and pointed out the worn carved heart and her initials.

"You did that?" he asked.

Nodding, she leaned back against the trunk. "I know it sounds silly, but I feel as if the little girl I used to be is looking on and she's disappointed. *She* wasn't going to let anyone but the man she'd love for ever kiss her. Fairytale stuff, I know…" She set her jaw and growled. "I wish I'd been born a boy."

"Because boys don't get pregnant? Not every man is like your father, Phoebe."

"You, for instance?"

She cringed at the acid in her tone. This wasn't Pace's fault. It wasn't anyone's…except perhaps her mother's.

"Yeah. Right," he said. "I'm so slick I managed to seduce you the first time we met."

She didn't smile at his joke. Who was he trying to fool? "The night we met there must have been at least a dozen women hanging off your every word. The next time I saw you there were even more. They were like ants on a sugar bowl. You could've had your pick."

His voice deepened. "But I'm not with any of them. I'm with you."

He pushed to his feet and came close. After combing

some hair back from her temple, he gently held her cheek. She thought he was going to kiss her again, and she was torn between desperately wanting him to and asking whether he'd listened to anything she'd said.

And then he did kiss her…tenderly…on her brow.

"It's been a big day," he said. "We'd better head back."

The breath left her body as her stomach sank. No one in the world could know her internal tug of war. She wanted to cast away all her doubts and experience everything she and Pace could share together. On the other hand, after today, she understood as she'd never understood before that she didn't want to give too much of herself—the way her mother had given way too much to that man.

But she wasn't fourteen any more. She was an adult who could look after herself. She should be able to rationalise those feelings. Sort them out and get on with it.

"I'm sorry—" she began, not really knowing what else to say.

"It's fine. Don't worry." He gave her arm a squeeze. "Come on. If we hurry, we can get back on the road before sunset."

He turned away to repack the hamper.

Phoebe watched, sick at heart, knowing precisely what he was thinking: that she was a nut. That Steve was right. She was a big fat dud.

As a young girl she'd wanted to find Prince Charming. When she was a teenager she'd been determined to stay away from men; she didn't want to know about emotions that might blind her to responsibility and common sense. Later she'd decided she only needed to keep clear of the wrong *kind* of man—love 'em and leave 'em types like her father. But recently…

Well, recently there'd been the list.

Find Mr Right Now. The guy with the magic touch.

But she was putting too much pressure on herself to make that happen. Perhaps she'd held back too much for too long? Maybe she ought to simply let it go and not dwell too much on being…incomplete?

She watched Pace, the way he moved with such animalistic grace—so fluid and hypnotic, even while doing something as banal as folding a blanket—and, no matter the demons knocking in her brain, she simply couldn't accept it. With Pace she *knew* she'd feel everything a woman was supposed to. The sparks, the fire, the furious euphoric release.

She wasn't talking about something as basic as an orgasm. She wanted to know about the genius of two people joining who connected on every intimate level in every intimate way. About a person's soul reaching a burning pinnacle and being reduced to ashes a heartbeat before it was reborn into something close to profound. An emotion, an experience, that could never be threatened or belittled or taken away even if the relationship wasn't meant to last for ever. She wanted to know she could feel that whole.

She couldn't let that go.

She had something to prove—not to Pace or to Steve or to the Tyler's Steam prudes of her childhood. What she had to prove she'd prove to herself. And, make no mistake, despite what had just happened, barring nothing, she'd prove it tonight.

* * *

From Phoebe's front door, Pace searched the endless plain. He coiled some fingers into his mouth and hurled out a long, loud whistle, then, straining to hear, waited for a response.

Where the hell *was* that dog?

After arriving back from their walk fifteen minutes earlier, Phoebe had assured him that Hannie would return soon enough. Then she'd set about unpacking the hamper, insisting he relax and that she'd do it herself.

She seemed affable enough, but...distracted. He couldn't blame her. What he'd learned this afternoon changed everything. He'd hoped to stay the night, but that was no longer on the cards. He still wanted her, nothing could change that, but from this point on it was advance in first gear all the way.

She'd had it tough as a kid. Phoebe didn't want to end up like her broken-hearted mother and so, if he had it right, she found it difficult to trust—herself or anyone else in that situation—and truly let go.

But she wanted to. That list at her apartment proved it. Still, nothing was going to happen tonight.

"I'll scout around," he suggested. "Hannie might be lost."

Phoebe flung the teatowel over her shoulder. "He'll be back soon. Take a seat while I finish up."

She bent forward from the hips, rearranging the crockery to fit the cups back in. His gaze followed her movements while she worked. As her rear in that white flowing dress tipped one way and then the other the length behind his zipper grew. There wasn't a man in existence who desired a woman more than he desired her at this moment. What a time to want to play Galahad.

From the shadowed doorway, he watched as she straightened. After stretching her back like a world-weary cat, she rummaged around in a drawer and found a rubber band. Holding the band between her teeth, she set about finger-combing her long silky hair up into a ponytail.

Beneath the bodice of the white dress her breasts bobbed as her fingers worked her hair higher and higher. He imagined how rosy the tips would be, how hot and delicious they'd feel and taste beneath his tongue. Between his teeth.

His erection throbbed and, uncomfortable, he rear-ranged his feet.

It was all he could do not to stride over, bring her into his arms, plunder her mouth with his and grip her palm over one very volatile, very hard place. Would she shriek back in horror, or melt like butter on a red-hot stove?

She stopped, frowned. When she darted a look his way and smiled, that rubber band still in her mouth and arms holding up all that hair, his stomach kicked with want and his gaze slid away.

Get it together, Davis. She might be the sexiest female on the planet, but he'd vowed to step back. If he couldn't do that, then he needed to step out.

Driving down a breath, he hooked a thumb towards the fields outside. "I'm going to find that dog."

"No."

Already heading out, he pulled up. Having dropped her hair, Phoebe was crossing the room to join him in the doorway. She slipped the rubber band over her wrist and searched a landscape patterned with deepening shades of purple and grey.

"When he's out playing," she said, "Hannie won't come even when *I* call. We'll just have to wait. I'll put the lights out too, except for the lamp. That should help."

"How?"

"If the lights are on he'll think there's still time to run around. Lights out, he'll race back, afraid to be left behind."

Pace rubbed his chin. Oddly enough, it made sense.

"I'm sorry," she said. "Holding you up like this. Especially…" Her gaze edged away. "Especially after what happened this afternoon."

An image of him holding her, kissing her passionately under that tree, gripped his imagination, and an even more dangerous heat flooded his veins.

"I want you to know—in case you didn't…" she smiled almost shyly "…I like the way you kiss."

He pressed his back against the jamb and groaned in his throat. She wasn't making this easy.

"Thanks," he said tightly. "Ditto."

She looked out, surveying the view again.

"Someone on the show last week explained a good kiss as 'the elixir of life'. But a recent report I read for research talks of kisses only in terms of foreplay."

He crossed and fastened his arms over his fast-beating heart. Foreplay was such an evocative word— particularly in the state he was in.

"On one of the first shows we did," she continued, "a contestant said she believed it all begins and ends with a kiss." She wound the rubber band off her wrist, set it between her teeth, and filed her fingers up through her hair to finish the job he'd interrupted a moment ago.

As she gazed out into the coming night, gathering silken hair high on her head, he stood, absorbed in the sight of that rubber band in her mouth…entranced by how lush and wet and inviting her lips looked in the rising moonlight. At some point he realised she was talking—something about her hair sticking to her back while she'd been working in the kitchen—and as her lips moved and unwittingly teased him the band fell from her mouth. Still holding her hair up, she let out a curse. Then, "Could you get that for me, please?"

He'd hop around on one leg and blow a plastic horn if she asked.

He hunkered down and spotted the band straight off, but then his gaze locked on her beautiful bare feet, her slim ankles, toned naked calves. The perfumed scent of her skin drifted into his lungs and his chest squeezed. What he wouldn't give to taste a deliberate line from her inside knee all the way up to her throat.

The sound of her voice filtered over the top of his head and unlocked his spellbound state.

"Can you see it?" she asked. "Feel around."

His fingers itched to reach out and do just that, but he bunched them tight and clamped shut his eyes. If he didn't know better, he'd think she was deliberately trying to drive him mad.

"Isn't that it?" she said. "Near my foot?"

A set of feminine toes, painted pink, edged out. A breeze blew in at the same time, and as her leg moved, the wind rippled up under her skirt. He caught a flash of creamy thigh and white panties, and at the same time her scent burrowed deeper under his skin, detonating a series of test explosions through his blood.

Releasing her hair, she hunkered down too. Waves of blond silk spilled over her shoulders while she searched the floor and then broke into a smile. "Here it is, silly." She pulled the rubber band like a miniature slingshot, flicked his forearm and then laughed.

He didn't laugh back. He was too engrossed in that pair of firm breasts that seemed to jut out and whisper, *touch me*. If he moved a single muscle it would be to gather her up and kiss her senseless.

Foreplay... Elixir...

Perspiration broke out on his hairline.

That mutt had better get back soon, or he'd lose it.

When she reached out and he felt her fingers lift through his hair every tendon in his body winched tight. Burgeoning doors he'd held closed for too long sprang open and the beast inside reared up. Whether she needed time or not, *this* was a very self-evident first move. No man could—or *should*—ignore such an obvious sign.

But as he leaned towards her she drew away. He saw what she was holding and his gut fell.

"A leaf," she said, inspecting the dry brown specimen. "Must've blown in on the breeze." She flicked the leaf. As the wind carried it away she hugged herself, and inadvertently pushed her breasts together. "In fact it's getting cold. Think I'll go pull on something to warm up."

While Pace shuddered out a barely controlled breath, Phoebe found her feet and navigated the couch. She flicked the switch on a lampstand, then moved to thumb off the kitchen light.

When she asked, "Do you know how to light a fire?"

a rush of heat pooled in his loins. *Someone in this house sure did.*

She nodded at the fireplace. "There's wood in the bin. Matches on the mantel."

She added, "You'll need a poker. There's one there but it's so heavy I can barely lift it."

He swallowed. Join the club.

Fixated upon the sway of Phoebe's butt while she ascended the stairs to the loft, Pace managed a Neanderthal grunt as his eyes rocked back and forth. When she'd disappeared from sight he slumped against the jamb. He only hoped she'd find something huge and ugly to wear. A fashion monstrosity that obliterated her figure under a cover of thick, hairy wool.

He crossed to the hearth. Dropping to one knee, he scrunched paper, shoved it under the wood, and set it alight. Weak blue-orange ribbons licked through the pile, within minutes catching the wood to cast a theatre of flickering shadows across the ceiling and walls.

Standing, he prodded the crackling logs with the poker, and watched sparks swirl like clouds of busy fireflies. He heaped on another log, then stood back and dusted his hands, somewhat satisfied. A bit of masculine industry and exertion and he felt halfway composed. He could get through this. He just needed to remember that while sex was the only thing on *his* mind, she'd waved the "proceed with caution" flag. More was the pity.

Out of the corner of his eye he caught a movement… the glittering prisms of Phoebe's gaze reflecting the fire's glow. When his eyes adjusted to the light, they fell clean out of his head.

This couldn't be.

Phoebe was relaxed, leaning against the stair railing...

Naked?

CHAPTER SEVEN

PACE shook his head to jostle his brain, readjusted his vision and looked again.

No, Phoebe wasn't naked. Not entirely. Although the only thing separating decency from the barest of facts was a set of sexy black lingerie.

Dropping back against the mantel, Pace scrubbed his eyes. When he refocused, Phoebe was still there, looking like a pin-up, propped at a lazy angle against the railing, one shapely leg bent, an arm posed casually above her head. Roughly teased hair sat high in a wild, messy bun.

His pulse-rate tripped out as she began to move, slinking down the stairs with an unmistakable feline prowess, dragging a black silk night-coat behind her.

"Pace, you look a little piqued." Her voice was as sweet and thick as a smear of whipped cream. "Did I catch you off-guard? I'm sure I told you I wanted to change." Mischief twinkled in her eyes, while a twinge of wicked amusement framed her mouth. "Haven't you heard? It's not polite to stare."

She moved the rest of the way down the stairs and joined him. By the dancing flames of the fire she arched a brow and dropped the coat before one red-lacquered fingertip reached out. About to touch his lips, it back-tracked to her own overstated pout. The tip disappeared, sucked into that hypnotic rouged vacuum, before gradually withdrawing to ride a slow circle around the rim of his own gaping mouth. His mouth automatically closed when her finger slipped between his lips, slipped back out, then—dear God—slipped back in again.

A hum of satisfaction vibrated from Phoebe's throat when she retracted her finger a final time, then trailed it from her jaw to the dip between her cupped breasts.

Pace shook himself again. Hard.

Nothing made sense right now except the wild thumping in his chest. What had got into her? Less than an hour ago, by that tree, she'd apologised for having to break off what had seemed to be going so well. She'd still been acting all butter-wouldn't-melt-in-her-mouth before she'd gone upstairs to "warm up". More like *strip down*.

But she sure as hell didn't look innocent now. She looked seriously sexy.

Still, there was something more lying behind the shadows in her gaze and the too-perfect pout of her lips. A hint that perhaps she wasn't as comfortable with this show as she might have him believe. But she was doing such a fine job it wouldn't take much to ignore it.

She dropped her gaze and studied his shirtfront before meekly handling its opening. When she twirled and tugged at the wiry hair at the vee, the fireball forming low in his gut swelled and almost shot free.

Pace pointed out, "You said you were cold."

"I'm heating up now, though," she purred. "How about you?"

He moved closer. "I'm about to boil over."

But she was already curling around his side, manoeuvring her body so it seemed each gliding inch made contact with some area of his anatomy. Behind him now, she fanned meaningful touches over his shoulders and back. Her fingers trailed lower, across his butt, then scooped between his denim-clad thighs to cup and squeeze.

Shuddering at a spike of pleasure, he made a grab for her hand, but she twined away again, slipping under his arm until she stood before him once more. A brush of satin—her cheek—nuzzled at his chest. Through the fabric of his shirt, sharp teeth nipped. On fire, he gritted his teeth against a groan of pure ecstasy.

His mind was sizzled mush, his body a mass of molten lust. This entire scene was mind-blowing, and while every brain cell still functioning told him not to question, Pace couldn't help but ask…

"What's going on?" Was she about to pull the pin again? Back off and make an excuse like earlier. "Is it safe to get excited?"

Her smile was ripe with promise. "Should you get excited? Definitely." Straightening, she urged up his shirt and, with his help, wrangled it over his shoulders and head. "Is it safe?" Each hand cupped a pec as her tongue, stiff and wet, tickled that still burning nipple. He felt her grin against his flesh. "That's something you'll need to decide for yourself."

She swept up the robe and whipped out its tie belt. Then she found his hands and joined the palms as if he were in prayer. After slotting them into her cleavage, she lashed his wrists together. She double-checked the knot before a dainty foot hooked the back of his ankles and she shoved him on the couch.

In freefall, he hit the cushions with an airy thud. A dizzy moment later she was kneeling over him, manipulating their positions until he lay on his back, arms bridged over his head. As if she were doing something as everyday as icing a cake, she straddled his chest and tied his cuffed hands to the lampstand.

Absorbing it all, Pace merely grinned.

He couldn't wait to see what came next.

Don't think. Just do it.

On the surface, she might appear to be completely in control, but underneath her sultry act Phoebe wasn't much better than a quivering bag of nerves.

She'd made her decision. No more false starts. No matter what, the next time Pace held her the kissing wouldn't stop until they'd gone all the way. Walking back to the cottage, she'd formed her plan. She'd primed the scene, talking with Pace in the doorway, then headed upstairs to change into the lingerie she'd brought with her from Sydney just in case.

But as she'd slinked down the stairs to rejoin Pace in the firelight flickering over the quiet walls, her anxiety had peaked to a near-crippling state and she'd very nearly backed out. Her palms had been so damp. Her stomach wouldn't quit rolling. Her knees had trembled enough to fold at any time.

She'd been committed to going forth and slaying those I'm-not-frigid dragons. But could she go through with something as outrageous as a striptease? If only she knew how it would play out. Would she make a complete fool of herself? Or, having thrown herself into the deep end without a lifejacket, would she at last find what had previously eluded her? An experience—a connection—that would once and for all release her and all she could be.

Now that she'd witnessed Pace's positive reaction the nerves weren't jittering quite so much. And she felt so incredibly aware. So alive! Still, she'd only just made it out the gate. The interesting, terrifying part was still to come.

With a merciless yank she made certain the rope lashing Pace's wrists to the lampstand was secure. Then, for good measure and an added tease, she leant forward, trailing two fingertips over the vein bulging on top of one masculine hand. She peered down over her black lace bra and, amazed she was actually doing this, meekly enquired, "Too tight?"

Pace blinked up with a mixture of arousal and expectation. "Just tight enough."

Beneath her spreadeagled thighs Pace shucked his wrists one way, then the other. The heavy base of the stand didn't budge; it weighed at least half a ton.

"Can't see how I can help this way, though," he said, and she shrugged.

"No help needed."

Remembering his advice from yesterday again—*don't think, just do it*—she twirled around until she sat facing his boots. Her heart pumping madly, she gradually fell forward, touched his toes, then arched slowly back, scraping her nails along two long stretches of denim. Her fingers came to rest on patches of burning skin either side of a concave navel. When those boots quivered, Phoebe took two deep breaths and then brought her mouth to his toned belly. The coarse hair tickling her chin, she kissed the square inch directly above his zipper. The flesh beneath her lips was on fire...the scent she caught was uncensored male.

Phoebe's core heated and throbbed.

"Everything under control down there?" Pace's voice had been dragged through the thickest molasses. "Want me to...uh—" she kissed him again and his hips bucked "—heel off my boots?"

She cast a lazy glance over her shoulder. "You can leave your boots on."

After easing off her perch, she stood before him, taking stock of the blood-pumping picture splayed out on her couch. She lapped up the magnificent male form...the shadows shifting with erotic languor over hard-muscled abs, biceps, chest. When her gaze connected with his, her heart leapt to her throat. She'd expected to see a certain wariness edging his expression. What she recognised in the focused gleam in his eyes was something else entirely.

Enjoyment—pure and simple. And challenge. He reminded her of a wild beast that was biding its time, waiting for the right moment to break free and claim a sweet reward all its own.

At her back, a log crumbled into the fire's ashes, and Phoebe was shaken out of her trance. Swallowing, she focused on taking her next step before any nerves could creep back in.

Moving to the CD-player, she made a selection, pressed "play" then let the soulful notes of a clarinet wash over her. Conjuring a provocative fluid motion, she threaded her fingers up through her hair to dislodge the single pin and release a waterfall of hair upon her shoulders. Then, ordering herself to give in to the music and the mood, she began to dance—to weave and stretch, roll and dip—a little stiffly at first.

But as the seconds wound into minutes she limbered up, and the tight knots in her stomach gradually took on a different form…a pulsing push and pull that started out as sparks igniting back and forth through her blood and then grew into something far more intoxicating.

Something clear and bright.

Listen to the music and let yourself go.

Her confidence building along with the heat in the room, Phoebe swayed away from the corner, arching and twirling, allowing herself only to *feel* in the immediate, smouldering present. When barely an arm's length separated her from Pace she closed her eyes again and absorbed the crisp dry air, as well as the symphony caressing her every move.

She felt it. *Was* it.

Desirable. Powerful.

Sexy.

Opening her eyes, she focused on her captive audience. Pace's nostrils flared like an animal testing the air as he concentrated on her performance.

Deliciously reckless now, she smiled. "You like to see a woman dance, Pace?"

A pulse pounded at the side of his throat.

"Some women."

Winding around to offer a rear view, she tucked a cheek into her shoulder. "*This* woman, Pace?"

Blue eyes gleamed in the shadows. "Yes, Phoebe. I like to see you dance."

Something in the deep focus of his tone stilled her for a beat. She felt locked in the power of his gaze and the message it seemed to convey. *My turn's coming.*

But then the music swelled and she was lost again, more aware with every chord of how deeply this act was affecting her—and Pace—on every level. It was as if she'd become another person…the person she'd always known she could be in the right situation. With the right man.

On a whim, she turned her back to him, hugged herself, and manufactured a pitiful attempt to reach her bra's clasp. "I can't seem to…" She pretended to stretch. "I can't seem to reach."

But rather than react Pace simply lay there, strangely unmoved.

Her swaying faltered as her stomach pitched and her heart began to pound a different beat. Why no reaction? Had she done something wrong? Something to turn him off?

As she edged around to face him Pace grimaced, arched his back, and let out a gut-wrenching oath. A harrowing feeling funnelled through her and Phoebe held her breath. What was happening? Clearly he was in pain. Was he having a heart attack? A stroke?

When he arched higher, grimaced harder, she rushed over and fell to her knees. His eyes were squeezed tight, his expression tortured.

She touched his cheek. "Pace, what's wrong?"

"Something…cutting into—" he cursed again "—back of neck."

Had she left a pair of manicure scissors on the cushions? She'd eaten dinner on this couch many times. Had a knife, lost in the join, stuck into his back?

She sent a hand in to tunnel behind his neck. He growled out again, louder this time. Desperate, she struggled to see around his mountainous shoulders.

"Right *there*," he let her know, as half her arm disappeared between his back and the couch.

Panic beating in her ears, she burrowed deeper, felt around. "I—I don't feel anything."

His face was inches from hers. Heartbeat hammering, she searched his eyes for a sign, for some instruction on what to do next. But of course she needed to get a knife, or scissors, hurry back, cut the tie and set him free. She needed to do it *now.*

About to bolt to the kitchen, Phoebe hesitated. Pace's expression had changed. Rather than pinched, his face now seemed strangely at peace. Make that supremely satisfied.

Her stomach clenched sickly around a dense ball when he smiled and the horrible truth dawned.

His sudden pain, the grimace, the moans…it had all been a trap. She'd been tricked!

Growling, she tried to yank her arm free. Stuck fast between the couch and his back, it wouldn't budge.

Pace's smile grew. "What do you intend to do now, Mata Hari?"

Her mind racing, she stammered, "I—I wasn't going to keep you tied up all night, I swear."

"And now?"

"Now you move and I'll cut you free."

In the firelight, she saw his eyes narrow. "What say we strike a deal? I'll let you go in return for a kiss."

"A *kiss*?"

She blinked. That was it? There had to be more to it than that.

"One kiss," he confirmed, reading her thoughts. "Now, bring your lips here, Phoebe. Bring them here *now*."

She bristled at his command. She was the one who

was supposed to be in charge here. But pins and needles were biting at her fingers, and his steely gaze told her he had no intention of relenting until she did as she was told.

She tried to come up with a plan, but there was only one that she half liked. If he wanted a kiss, she'd give him one to remember.

Wishing she felt as confident as she had moments ago, she lowered her head and let her mouth hover for a titillating moment above his. Then she grazed her lips over his chin, his raspy jaw. A flurry of heightened sensation flew through her middle and she swallowed a breath, enjoying the sizzling aftershock to her core. She waited for his reaction…waited for his mouth to reach up and unreservedly claim hers. Instead, he nipped her, gently imprisoning her bottom lip between his teeth.

She yelped—out of shock, not pain. But then his tongue started to move, stroking the wet sweep of her lower lip, laving its sensitive mound, and darkest pleasure rolled through her like the lethal shadow of a gathering wave. Eyes drifting shut again, she quivered out an involuntary sigh and helpless, trembling, waited for his next move.

First his head angled, gifting barely-there kisses to her chin. Then his mouth deliberately closed over hers, his day-old growth grazing languidly back and forth against the edge of her jaw as he drew her in. Her every thought, every memory, every doubt, lifted and drifted far away.

His tongue swept inside her mouth, running over its roof, exploring its unabashed welcome. And then he wasn't kissing her any more. *She* was kissing *him*. Kissing him with everything she had and wanted to give. The feeling spiralled until she couldn't siphon in enough air. Could this possibly get any better?

As her free hand traced the line and movement of his working jaw, the aching burn, low and deep inside her, intensified. The sensation was surreal. A completely different plane. Her system surged with a series of dark-light, sharp-soft, tender-deep thrills. It was eternal. It was time standing still.

And just imagine when they finally made love…

When Pace gently broke the kiss a little of the tension leaked out of her. But as their lips parted Phoebe didn't open her eyes. This break was to catch their breath, to refuel their engines before the finale. Then she was going back to kiss him again.

Going back for more.

His laugh—a low, devilish sound—froze Phoebe's thoughts. When he laughed again her eyes sprang open, and her blood warmed with a different kind of heat. The realisation was as profound as a mountain toppling, a tidal wave crashing, and as the understanding compounded her stomach looped into a thousand knots.

He was *laughing* at her. Laughing at how easily he'd taken control.

But at this point did it matter? This coming-apart-at-the-seams scenario was precisely what she'd wanted. She might have lost control, but wasn't that a good thing? The outcome she'd been hoping for?

Feeling somewhat pleased with herself, she fought the urge to lick her lips. "Well, was that kiss enough for you?"

"Oh, yeah." His smile shone. "That was definitely kiss enough."

"Now that's settled, would you kindly keep your end of the bargain and release my arm?"

He raised a brow. "I don't think so. I like you where you are."

She frowned. "But you said—"

"I lied."

"That's not fair!"

"I suppose it isn't. But then neither is you tying me up." He grinned crookedly. "Not that I mind."

She nibbled her bottom lip. "I suppose you want an explanation?" About the strip, about the tying up.

"That would be nice, but not necessary."

"On our way back this afternoon," she began, before she could chicken out, "I made up my mind to—"

"To find your 'Mr Right Now'?"

Her mouth fell open. "How did you—?"

His voice lowered. "Phoebe, I saw your list."

A fire lit in her chest and swept up her neck and over her cheeks. She could easily have been embarrassed into her next lifetime, but now she had other priorities—like saving her fingers before they dropped off from lack of circulation.

"Can we please continue this conversation after you get off my arm?"

"So you can leave me here like this?" He shook his head.

She huffed out a breath. Time to point out the obvious. "Either you shift and free me, or we stay here, like this, all night."

"You've had your fun, Phoebe." His face and tone darkened. "Now it's time I had mine."

She was about to point out his prostrate manacled

position. She might not be in charge, but neither, exactly, was he. Then she felt his biceps strain, his chest expand.

A second later the tie's stitching ripped apart.

CHAPTER EIGHT

RELISHING the startled look on Phoebe's face, Pace focused his energy on snapping what remained of his silk chain. Adrenaline pumping, he stored some oxygen, clenched his teeth and *pulled*.

His hands flew forward and apart. Continuing the movement, he looped his arms over Phoebe's head. After she'd wriggled her arm free from under his back he tugged her relentlessly close, openly smiling at her wide-eyed surprise. He hadn't spoilt her fun. He'd merely spiced it up.

"You'd like to say something?" he asked.

Phoebe barely managed a squeak. With an exaggerated hug that flattened her chest snug against his, he glanced around the room, as if they were a couple about to christen their new home.

"Yes, indeed." He exhaled heartily. "This sure is cosy."

He heard her swallow. "Pace…you can let me up now."

He grinned. Not a chance.

Seemed she'd decided to go through with taking care of her wish list after all. Oh, she'd had him fuddled for a while, not knowing if he were coming or going, when she'd teased him under that tree and then later in the doorway. But there was no misunderstanding this time. With this scintillating bump and grind routine she'd let him know precisely what she had in mind, and he would do everything within his power to help her out.

But when he angled up to kiss her again she broke free and scrambled off the couch. Her chest rose and fell as she tried to catch her runaway breath. Beneath the black lace bra her nipples called to him, dark and deliciously beaded.

"This isn't…isn't what I planned," she panted.

He sent her a lopsided grin. "Nothing beats a good surprise."

He slid to his feet and moved towards her with an intentionally predatory gait. He didn't give her time to think or back out. He brought her into the merciless circle of his arms and kissed her—hard, without apology—precisely the way she wanted him.

The moment his mouth took hers, she surrendered, quivering delectably against him. Several heady heartbeats later she rose up on her toes and returned his passion, stroke for blessed stroke. Her tongue parried with his as her fingers drew up over his shoulders, up through his hair. With her breasts pushed against his chest, he felt her heart beating a million to one.

Her skin felt on fire…her back, waist, the amazing curve of her hips. Without breaking mouth-to-mouth contact, Pace scooped her up off the floor and into his arms, then moved a few blind steps to the rug. There he carefully laid her down and then, taking a moment, drew slightly away.

The rug was a snowy aura surrounding her gloriously tight body. Her smile was dreamy and her eyes

were dark, slumberous and wanting. When she reached
to trace the line bracketing his mouth, he pressed his
lips to her palm and buried his face in the sweet berry
fragrance of her hair.

A pulse drummed at the side of her throat. His lips
brushed its fluttering beat, and that drugging sensation heightened, driving white-hot flames through his
blood. He needed to touch her—everywhere and all at
once. He wanted to take her to the ultimate, unbearable
brink and have her teeter there for as long as humanly
possible. More than anything he wanted to show her
how good it could be.

What making love was all about.

He manoeuvred out of his jeans, his shirt, then joined
her again, lying front to front. She at once coiled a silky
thigh over his hip. When her hand found his erection,
as if waving a wand she turned solid rock into a span
of high-tensile steel. In the fireglow he slipped down
one bra strap, his touch sculpting down to expose her
breast. After his thumb grazed and teased its tip, he
lowered his head and drew her deep into his mouth.

With his tongue circling the peak, he groaned out
his pleasure while Phoebe gripped his shoulder and
snatched in a lung full of air. When his tongue flicked
back and forth, then circled again, she arched against
him, holding on with an intensity that ended with beads
of sweat breaking free at his every pore.

Amazing that through that heavy haze of arousal he
remembered to be responsible. Feeling around, he found
his discarded jeans and a condom in the back pocket.
Shifting his mouth from one breast to the perfect other,
he extracted the rubber and rolled the protection on.
Then he moved back up to meet her mouth, kissing her

with an incontestable force as his fingers slid down her flat tummy, beneath her panties, and through the satin tangle at the apex of her thighs. When she shuddered out a rapt sigh, his touch slid further and curled inside.

His erection shuddered and hardened more.

She was so warm and wet and gloriously ready.

His blood on fire, he snatched several hungry kisses from her lips, her chin, then pressed his hips in against hers, imagining the moment of ecstasy when her inner walls would contract around more than his finger. His breath laboured, he tasted a seductive line down the curve of her throat while adjusting his stroke to draw a moist, slow circle around the nub at the top of her sex. She shivered violently. He grinned against her throat and circled again.

When her pelvis began to rotate against the movements of his hand, fresh dampness broke down the line of his back. His throat thick with want, he dragged her lace panties down to the knee, then whipped them completely off. His mouth found her breast again and he matched the rhythm of his swirling tongue with his concentrated caressing down below. When he applied a slip more pressure to both place, her body jerked up, lifting higher…higher…before she tensed.

He felt every string in her body stretched tight. Sensed her every fibre on the brink and aching for release. Gently he tugged at her nipple with his teeth and lightly pinched her most sensitive spot, then pinched and tugged a little harder…a little faster. When he drew the bud of her breast deeply into his mouth she gasped, grabbed his head and his hand and, groaning out his name, held on tight.

Pressing up, she convulsed countless sublime times. Every muscle braced, he held on to her, caressing her, murmuring her name as she rocked against him, gripping the rug with one hand and his arm with the other. Still in the throes, she rolled her head from one side to the other as the waves washed on.

Gradually the tremors ebbed. Her sighs were long and satisfied, and as she dragged the damp hair from her brow and floated down from her rise Pace eased himself over and on top. He murmured against the shell of her ear and pushed carefully, needfully inside. As his length filled her a hot rush of pleasure swept over his skin and a barrage of burning arrows shot to his groin. She felt so soft and tight and infinitely feminine.

Losing himself to sensation, he closed his eyes and curled his arms around her head. Nuzzling against her temple, he worked his way in and blissfully out, repeating the action until the rhythm left his mind exquisitely blank to anything other than her body joined with his.

Groaning low in his throat, he held her closer.

All he could think of…all he wanted…was Phoebe.

Her nails trailed up the sides of his back, leaving tracks of goosebumps as they curved around his shoulders, then clawed lightly like a kneading kitten at his chest. When he set his teeth and thrust in to the hilt she arced up, drinking from his lips while he kissed her back, heart and soul. He gripped her hip, fastened her calf over his thigh, then thrust again and again until his scalp tingled and the urge to unload was more powerful and wild than a stampede of stallions.

She whispered in his ear, dug her heel into his thigh.

Her parted lips traced up his damp throat, and as her hot breath teased his skin her teeth grazed and nipped his jaw.

Enough.

An almighty thunderbolt cracked. He clenched down, cupped her face, and kissed her mindlessly while he spasmed and found his own sweet release.

Early the next morning Phoebe woke with a start and a thrilling flash from the night before. She remembered lovemaking that had gone on into the early hours. She remembered tender words and the thrilling way Pace had brought her to climax again and again. Now all she wanted was to relive those wild, mindless moments. Tingling all over, dying to see his face, she carefully rolled onto her side.

Before they'd fallen asleep in each other's arms Pace had recovered from her loft a quilt and pillows. Asleep beside her, now Pace began to stir. Quietly propping up on an elbow she drank in his profile—sweeping dark lashes, strong straight nose, that full bottom lip she'd kissed and kissed but could never get enough of. That inky-black hair and bronzed super-toned body...

At this moment, asleep, Pace was more dazzling and desirable than he'd ever been before.

The fireplace was a bed of cold ash where earlier it had burned like a veritable inferno. Never in her life had she known a more consuming heat. Never had she enjoyed a more feverish time. Making love to Pace was everything she'd hoped it would be. Everything and more.

After all the angst and doubt she'd finally discovered it was true. Multiple fireworks *could* explode when a woman made love with the right man. Not just fireworks. The entire world had ceased to exist. She wouldn't have cared if plum-sized diamonds had begun to fall from the sky. What she and Pace had shared last night was all-consuming. So strong, so intense, the sensations and emotions he'd brought out in her were the most achingly beautiful she'd ever known.

Now the workings of her body hummed and heated anew, begging her to be selfish, to reach out and touch him…wake him. As her gaze roamed his bare shoulder and strong corded arm, her lips burned to brush the hollow of his throat and kiss a slow, blissful line from his chest to the ridges of his exposed six-pack.

She wanted him to fill her again so badly she felt faintly woozy with the need. With him she'd felt confident, beautiful, desirable and…

Secure.

Pace sucked in a rousing breath and stretched one strong arm high above his head. His eyes blinked open, his brow furrowed at his surrounds, then recognition sparked in his eyes and he tipped towards her. His smile illuminated the room more brightly than any morning light. With a playful sexy growl, he leaned close and nipped her ear.

"Morning, gorgeous." He circled the lobe with his tongue, then blew gently, and a wondrous awakening shiver shimmied through her. "Did you sleep well?"

"I know *you* did." Cocooned in a warm sense of belonging, she burrowed in and wrapped herself around all that marvellous masculine heat. "I don't think you moved all night."

His lips grazed her brow. "After the third time you'd exhausted me." He dragged her up against him, closer and higher, until their noses and foreheads touched. "But I'm all rested now."

Sighing, Phoebe fell into the practised magic of his kiss—a gift that was predominantly natural but to some extent must also be acquired. His skill in the bedroom was an art form. He might try to play down his obvious fascination with women—and their fascination with him—but she wasn't fooled. Heaven knew how many times he'd been in just this situation, in bed with someone he'd met less than a handful of times, immeasurably pleased with how successfully he'd brought her to life with his finesse.

Deep into the kiss, her eyes closed, Phoebe had no regrets. She'd set out to play with fire last night and she'd enjoyed every minute. But after today she needed to leave those flames behind. She'd proved what she'd set out to prove, but she didn't intend to make a habit of it. Pace Davis would be way too easy to fall in love with, and more than common sense said he wasn't the kind to reciprocate.

Men who could play the field so effortlessly—with such dedication and relish—normally kept their hearts. It went with the bad boy territory. Now that he'd accomplished what he'd set out to achieve—now that he'd bedded her all through the night—she'd bet that he'd quit the chase and move on quickly enough. It wasn't as if he wouldn't have a string of women wanting to take her place.

But when his mouth continued to lay its claim over hers Phoebe didn't resist. She had no intention of making these last hours together anything but unforgettable.

Right Now wasn't over just yet.

CHAPTER NINE

"Roses." Sam Campbell smacked a spanner into Pace's outstretched hand, planted the seat of his navy blue overalls on a nearby workhorse and stated, "Women love roses."

Pace manoeuvred his head out from beneath the hood of the classic Mercedes that he'd worked on the best part of the day. Stretching his back, he gave Sam's suggestion some serious thought.

Was it that simple? A dozen roses and the wall Phoebe had erected between them this past week would crumple and disappear into the sunshine?

Sam knew Pace better than anyone. They'd done college together, had white-water rafted a few times and jumped out of planes on occasion. Every Tuesday they played pool at Pitt Street. Pace trusted this man with his life, and had trusted him today with the story of his rollercoaster weekend with the delectable, frustrating as hell Phoebe Moore.

He'd explained how that Saturday at Tyler's Stream had gone from promising to dead to *electrifying* in a matter of hours. The night they'd spent together had been beyond compare—he believed for both of them. When he and Phoebe had driven back to Sydney they'd stopped at Brodricks and swapped the Aston for her contracted BMW, which had arrived. Then he'd kissed her goodbye and, waving, she'd driven off. From that time to this, other than one bizarre phone conversation when she'd told him that she was busy over the next few days and would call when she had more time, Phoebe had refused to pick up and speak to him.

He was confused, certainly. Annoyed? You bet. The time for playing those kind of *you-can't-catch-me* games was long over.

"I fronted up at the television studios," he told Sam, weighing his wrench in his hand. "But she never seems to be there. And they didn't record her show the Saturday just past. I've even knocked on her apartment door." Perhaps louder than he should have. That old bat Mrs G had popped her jet-rinse head out through her door and grumbled that her young neighbour was away visiting friends.

Pace swiped his brow with the back of his forearm.

Was Phoebe embarrassed that she'd let herself go with him so completely? She needn't be. What they'd shared had not only been better than sensational, it had been inevitable. He'd told her as much. Inevitable, and far from over.

Cursing, he dropped the wrench into the toolbox.

What was she playing at? Did she want him to do loops chasing her? Did she think he'd give up?

"I'm no expert on the workings of a woman's mind," Sam announced, unwrapping his ham and cheese on rye, "but maybe she's hanging out for more."

"Hanging out for what?"

Sam shrugged. "A proposal?"

Pace's blood stopped flowing, then he hacked out a raucous laugh. "Who mentioned marriage?"

The office trainee was striding into the garage. His teenage shoulders pinned back, he handed Pace a memo. His mind still on Phoebe, Pace accepted the note and absently thanked the kid.

"I don't want to *marry* her," Pace announced, scrunching the memo in his hand. "I just want to talk to her."

"Talk?" With a wry grin, Sam bit into his sandwich and chewed. "Uh-huh."

Pace gave his friend a look, then remembered the memo and flicked open the crumpled page.

From: Nick Brodrick
Pace, due to cutbacks, regrettably the penthouse in Darling Harbour will no longer be available for your personal use. It's been decided that the facility will be—

When Pace growled and screwed the paper into a tight wad, Sam asked, "What's up?"

"My brother trying to box me in yet again."

Would it always be like this? A continual battle? One brother trying to upstage the other? Sometimes he thought it might be better to simply walk away and leave Nick to his spoils. He'd thank God every day for not having to see Nick's face and be reminded of the final tip of the scales that had cast him out and hoisted Nick Junior into the top chair.

But bowing out wasn't an option. This company was a part of him. Nick would never throw in the towel either. The brothers had always duelled and would continue to do so, Pace feared, until one of them fell and couldn't get back up.

But he wouldn't waste any more brain cells on that battle today.

His brow furrowed, he lobbed the paper ball from one hand to the other as he paced to the far side of the garage and back.

"This thing with Phoebe is doing my head in," he admitted. And he wasn't completely certain why. If he boiled it all down, Phoebe was just another woman. There were lots of women in the world. In this city, for that matter. Women who wouldn't give him this kind of runaround.

He over-armed the paper ball and it landed in the bin. "If I was smart I'd forget her."

Sam brushed his hands free of crumbs. "But you can't?"

Exhaling, Pace sank down heavily beside his friend. "Right."

"Ever consider the possibility that you might have fallen in love?"

"Fallen in—" Shaking his head, Pace strode back to peer, unseeing, into the engine cavity, his hands clenched either side of the grille. "That's the most ridiculous thing you've ever said."

Sam sounded reflective. "I haven't been in love since sixth grade, when Kelly McCormick held me down behind the gymnasium and gave me the biggest, sweetest snog I've ever received. For a ten-year-old, Kelly sure could kiss."

His jaw tight, Pace kept his nose near the oil stick. "Nice story. But I'm not looking to swim the English

Channel, Sam. I just want to splash around and enjoy the water."

Admittedly, that water was damn fine. To date, the *finest*.

He'd never forget the way his body had simmered with unrefined need when Phoebe had danced and dipped for him that night. Thinking about her warm tongue delving around in his mouth, flicking over his skin, sent the constant tightening in his loins into overdrive.

Straightening, he cleared his throat and eased down the Merc's hood.

"Phoebe and I are beyond compatible in the bedroom," he confessed. "But no one said anything about *love*."

The word itself made him feel all itchy and uptight.

Sam kept on studying him, chewing the last of his ham on rye, his coal-black eyes looking unconvinced.

Grunting, Pace waved his friend off. Ah, what did he know?

But he clicked his cellphone from his belt. A walk down the aisle was out of the question. He was too young, too free. They barely *knew* each other. But roses...

He punched in directory assistance for the number of a florist.

Roses he could do.

As the stretch limousine pulled up on the glittering forecourt of an exclusive inner city building, Phoebe clutched the evening bag to her chest and tried to control the team of nerves playing jump rope in her belly.

It wasn't too late to pull out of this rendezvous. She could inform the driver she'd made a mistake and ask could he please take her straight back home.

But now that she'd come this far—feeling like Cinderella arriving at the ball—she owed it to herself to see what other surprises lay in store. She owed it to Pace, too. She'd thought he'd give up once he'd won his prize. Thought he'd grow tired of calling when she was constantly unavailable. Wrong. His efforts to see her again had only grown—and to heights that must have cost a small fortune.

She could admit she was flattered by the attention, but not enough to fool herself into believing this was anything more than it was. An encore. Pace was a ladies' man. He'd had a good time that night in her cottage. He wanted to enjoy those same highs again.

Gathering her courage, Phoebe raised her chin.

The naked truth was…so did she.

Looking beyond the limo's window into the building's glittering foyer, Phoebe slipped one of the cards Pace had sent her today back into her evening purse. A moment later the car's back passenger door swung open and the chauffeur assisted her out with gentlemanly grace. After brushing down the folds of her aqua silk gown, she pivoted on her matching high heels, hunting her surrounds for signs of her date.

She held her knotting stomach.

Where was Pace hiding?

From inside the hotel Pace gazed on, and he liked what he saw.

Phoebe's gown was cut daringly low at the back, and her silken hair sparkled in the moonlight with a thousand tiny diamantés. When a sudden gust eddied down the sidewalk, collecting a mini-whirlwind of leaves that funnelled around the fall of her skirt, it lifted the airy fabric enough to reveal a pair of slender ankles that Pace knew intimately. After rearranging her swirling gown, Phoebe stepped towards the chauffeur and must have asked a question—at which he drew a playful finger across sealed lips.

Pace's smile heated his chest. He was glad he'd followed Sam's advice. Glad he'd embellished it to the degree that he had. If a dozen red roses and a card would make Phoebe smile, why not go the whole hog and send twelve *dozen* dozen? He'd organised with the florist for the bouquets to arrive every twenty minutes at the studio. At six o'clock Phoebe had rung to accept his invitation to dinner. He'd told her to expect her ride at eight. Dress was formal.

Ted, the doorman, who'd been standing close by awaiting orders, slanted his head conspiratorially.

"Now, sir?"

Pace straightened. "Yes, Ted. Now."

The uniformed man shunted back his embossed jacket shoulders and started off.

The Brodricks penthouse, with its impressive city views, imported marble decor and quality furnishings, was usually kept vacant, ready at a moment's notice should one of Brodricks' clients visit and need accommodation. At other times it was free for Nick or Pace's personal use. Since returning home, however, Pace had felt more comfortable in his own home, which sat on a cliff overlooking the world's most beautiful harbour. But Nick's memo yesterday had turned his screws one notch too tight.

He would use this penthouse, and anything else related to Brodricks, any damn time he pleased—and if Nick wanted him to ask permission his brother would be waiting until lolly-pink was his favourite colour.

Outside, Ted introduced himself to Phoebe, then escorted her through soaring glass doors into the building. The subtle sway of her gown was nothing short of hypnotic. She'd looked fabulous in her Tyler's Stream casual white dress, edible in that black lingerie, but at a pinch Pace preferred her in evening wear. The way she held herself, the way she glided and glowed…it stole his breath away.

As his girl swept into the expansive marble foyer, Ted bowed off and Pace in his white dinner jacket stepped up. Spotting him, Phoebe froze, then released a dazzling smile while he closed in.

"I was hoping I wouldn't feel overdressed," she said, her eyes glistening beneath the lights.

"You're dressed to perfection."

Her cheeks flushed and she tilted her chin. "The flowers were unbelievable. Thank you."

"Glad you liked them."

"I can't imagine how much they cost." Her brow creased. "You shouldn't have wasted so much money."

"You liked them." *She was here.* "It wasn't wasted."

The flowers were just the beginning.

When his hand cupped her elbow, his chest swelled. "I hope you're hungry."

As they began to walk, she threw a curious glance around. "Where are we eating? This building has more than one restaurant, doesn't it?"

When she was about to enquire further, he placed a hushing finger to her parted lips. He didn't want to spoil the surprise.

"Follow me."

After they'd entered a lift, he hit the top floor button and a few moments later was leading Phoebe out onto the carpet of red and gold which blanketed the extensive private foyer of the penthouse floor. He pushed open the door, and the dulcet tones of violin strings drifting on the evening air washed over them.

Curious, Phoebe filed in ahead.

Her fingers trailed over the filigree lacing of an ornate mirror. She gaped at the collectors' pieces of post-modern sculpture housed safely within separate alcoves. She gripped her throat when he escorted her over a glass brick bridge under which dozens of over-sized goldfish glimmered within their mother-of-pearl moat. Gazing up as they alighted, she sighed at the classic Swarovski chandelier.

"Pace, how can you afford all this? Even for one night—?"

Her words ran dry when she spotted the string quartet in a far corner of the curved room decorated entirely in white. Four cheery grey heads dipped in greeting, while bows wove musical magic across violin strings.

Pace stole a sidelong look at her amazed expression and his chest expanded as he grinned. Three years ago he might have put together a party—themed, perhaps—with loud music and cocktails flowing. But now, given the company, this was far more his speed. The added touches were well worth it. He felt the sparks of excitement shooting off her. What was money if you couldn't enjoy it and have special people enjoy it with you?

And Phoebe was indeed special.

Phoebe was speechless. This apartment was light years beyond amazing. The fish, that gorgeous chandelier right out of a storybook, the string quartet!

Light-headed, Phoebe realised Pace was waiting for her beside open balcony doors. Ducking around the filmy curtain he held back, she moved out onto a massive balcony.

Beyond the carved stone railings a blanket of night lights twinkled and the subdued noise of traffic filtered up from far below. The balcony was alive with ribbons of scarlet bougainvillaea and a delicious aroma that sent Phoebe's tastebuds into a frenzy. To her left, a long table was lined with heated *bains maries* and artistic arrangements of colourful fruit, seafood and salads. A veritable *feast*.

A feast for two.

Crossing to stand beside her, Pace looked every bit the debonair playboy in that jacket. The magnificent line he cut, so tall and suave and commanding…she couldn't help but think that he'd been born to don a dinner suit.

On a white linen tablecloth silver cutlery and crystal flutes sparkled, care of flickering patio torches. Pace shrugged out of his jacket, and as he turned to rest it over a nearby chair Phoebe's gaze sailed to the symmetry of his back. His shirt strained against the jostle of working muscles, and she imagined the smooth, hot flesh beneath the fabric, as well as the subtle smell of sandalwood that she'd enjoyed during their ride in the lift.

She inhaled a shivery breath.

This night was bound to be one to remember.

When Pace faced her again, she gathered herself and smiled as he retrieved an impressive bottle of champagne from its ice bucket. He filled the chilled flutes and she tingled to her toes at the high-pitched ping when the crystal accidentally touched as he delivered her glass and an ice-cold flute pressed into her palm.

"I'd like to propose a toast," he said.

A pulse fluttered in her throat as she raised her glass. "A toast?"

His hooded gaze grew intense. "To the music and to our second dance together."

As her heart thudded, he clinked his glass to hers and sipped. He waited for her to taste the bubbles too, then took her glass, set it upon the table next to his, and folded her within the steamy circle of his arms.

Phoebe remembered again the hot thrill of his kisses, and her pulse-rate kicked up a notch. When his hot palm slid down her bare back and came to rest above the rise of her behind she bit her lip to stem a sigh. Then he began to move to the music and her body reacted instinctively, matching his step, flaming to life in response to the subtle magic of his moves.

"Are you okay with tonight being a private affair?" he asked, slow dancing her around in an intimate circle, his handsome face so confident and so close to hers.

"Depends." She arched a brow, not wanting to give away the fact that she was melting at a rapid rate. "Do you do this often?"

His lips touched her ear and he whispered, "Never."

She smothered a sigh. A foolish part of her wanted to believe him.

She looked into his eyes and tried not to swoon. "I thought you'd give up," she admitted.

"Trying to see you again?" His eyes sparkled in the torchlight. "Not a chance."

Her pulse pounded through the thousand pathways of her blood, leaving her giddy. Taking her higher. Five minutes and already things were moving quickly. She wanted everything to slow down, to savour every moment, and yet another part of her wanted to fast forward and once again know the feel of his mouth capturing hers.

His brow pinched. "Why didn't you return my calls, Phoebe?"

A shaft of guilt fell through her and she dropped her gaze. "I told you. I was busy last week."

"Too busy for this?" He brushed his mouth over her brow and instantly her breasts grew hot and heavy... full and tender.

Searching his eyes, she took the plunge. "I'm not too busy tonight."

Before picking up the phone and calling him Phoebe had made a deal with herself. If he was so determined to see her again she would meet with him, even *sleep* with him, but she wouldn't let herself get hung up on "what comes next". She'd vowed to keep a tab on her feelings and, subsequently, keep them in line. She could only guess how many women had thought themselves in love with the delectable Pace Davis over the years. He would be any woman's catch… But he was still single, wasn't he?

Clearly he wasn't looking for anything serious. Nothing permanent. But right now, the way her head was spinning and her heart was drumming, she too was happy to enjoy whatever lay ahead in the very immediate, intimate future.

His gaze roaming her face, he took in her reply and then, with a slow smile, pressed her closer, moving them both to the music.

"Do you have to go to work in the morning?"

She knew what he was asking—that she stay the night—and the thought flooded her belly with a hot pool of desire. She tried to mask her excitement with a light laugh and a flippant remark.

"You don't muck around, do you?"

"Where you're concerned?" With a knuckle, he tipped up her chin and skimmed his lips over hers. "Not any more."

She drew in a shaky breath. Her thoughts were whirling, but she wouldn't let him know how deeply his seductive voice, his skilled moves, were affecting her. She didn't want to dissolve into a quivering mass of hopeless want.

At least not yet.

"Good thing we have four elderly chaperons inside," she teased, and a wicked gleam shone in his eyes.

"You feel unsafe with me?"

"Unsafe isn't the word."

"Vulnerable, then?"

She thought about lying, but said instead, "Yes. A little."

His hot fingertips trailed her bare back, and as his other hand squeezed hers his smile widened.

Phoebe paused at a thought. "Pace, you're not thinking of borrowing my trick and tying me up, are you?"

"You know I prefer your hands free."

An image seeped into her mind…her hands on his hips, her mouth busy and in love with its task. Her core contracted, and her eyes drifted closed as she quivered with deepest longing, inside and out.

His husky voice brushed her hair. "Perhaps we should skip dinner."

She forced open her eyes and found his smouldering gaze fastened on her lips. Her heart clamouring, she tried to keep up her bravado, pretend she was as confident as he was. She was nowhere near. But that didn't mean she wanted to stop.

"You're not hungry?" she asked.

"Not hungry." He tucked her pelvis against his. "Ravenous."

"Well, then," she said, sounding breathy but unable to do anything about it, "what's for entrée?"

His eyes darkened.

"You."

She laughed softly, but inside she was shaking. The things he said, the way he looked at her…he didn't have to do a whole lot more to send her spiralling out of this galaxy.

"All I've thought about these past days," he murmured, moving to the music again, "is kissing you."

"I didn't realise I'd made such an impression," she jibed, and his eyes flashed with devilment.

"The hell you didn't."

His hand climbed until his warm palm reached her nape. His fingers twined in her hair and he urged her head back at the same time as his mouth closed over hers.

All those heady feelings came rushing back—the euphoria, the weak, wonderful throb of molten want winding through her blood. But the intensity was a thousand times stronger than a week ago. Truth was, she'd been unable to think of anything other than kissing *him* again too, and as his grip tightened on her arm and his tongue delved deeper Phoebe willingly surrendered to the thrill and the incomparable power of this amazing man's kiss.

When his mouth broke from hers gently, almost tenderly, his hooded eyes were dark and filled with intent.

He inhaled, satisfied. "I liked our dance," he murmured. "I could dance with you all night."

She tried but failed to catch her breath. Her every sense was zinging, neon bright. If he even *touched* her down there, there was every chance she might explode.

Fighting the urge to flatten herself against him, she swallowed another breath.

"If we dance all night the food will go cold."

He mock frowned. "We can't have that." Her hand in his, he led her to the banquet table. "No waiters. This evening, *madame*, I will serve."

Phoebe's mouth hooked up. Oh, she liked the sound of that.

"We have a selection for starters," Pace pointed out. "Are you a shellfish fan? Lobster? Oysters?"

Phoebe spotted a glass bowl of fruit and her taste-buds leapt to life. "I love strawberries."

Pace took his time choosing the biggest and reddest. While Phoebe waited she guessed his next move: bringing the strawberry to her lips and inviting her to eat it from his fingers. When he found a large plate and set the fruit in the centre Phoebe's heart sank. She'd been expecting something more...erotic. As if to compensate a little, he reached for a pourer of liquid chocolate and set that on the plate, too.

Phoebe's mouth watered. Her ideal combination.

He presented the plate, and she drenched the strawberry in thick dark chocolate. When she bit it, the mix of chocolate and fruit exploded in a heavenly cocktail on her tongue. Closing her eyes, she hummed and chewed and finally swallowed. After running her tongue over her lips, she popped the rest of the strawberry into her mouth. She'd brought her fingers close to lick their tips when she noticed Pace's expression.

With a slight breeze ruffling his hair, he looked both relaxed and fascinated. His gaze was drifting lower, down from her mouth to feather over the light fabric of her bodice. Beneath the aqua silk her nipples tingled, growing hard and hot beneath his stare. As her breathing picked up again his gaze trailed higher, to fuse with hers, its ascent leaving a sizzling path in its wake.

"You like sweet things?" His voice sounded irresistible and dark, like the chocolate lingering on her tongue.

She managed a careless shrug. "It's a weakness."

"Then you'll like this."

He heaped a portion of a meringue creation onto a

plate. Blueberries and passionfruit toppled off a crest of whipped cream as he presented it to her.

But he was ahead of himself. "Pace, Pavlova's a dessert."

"Yes, it is. Now..." The curve of his grin, the timbre of his voice, was mesmerising. "Close your eyes."

Inside, the quartet began another tune, this piece more lilting and evocative. Feeling carried away, she leaned back against the dinner table, held the edge either side, and willingly did as he bade.

In the darkness, the first thing Phoebe knew was the sugary smell. She guessed he'd scooped a helping of meringue onto a spoon and held it before her mouth. Tempted, she almost flicked out her tongue for a taste, but swiftly put that impulse aside.

She didn't want to seem too eager.

"Okay," he murmured, "open your mouth."

The delicious ache building in her stomach contracted at the quiet power of his words, and, compelled to do precisely as she was told, she opened up.

"Wider, Phoebe. Open wider."

A fire lit low in her stomach. Lifting her chin, she opened more.

What she guessed was a dessert spoon clicked against her teeth, then a dreamy blend of sugar and cream assailed her senses. As she tasted the confection she felt it too. The soft and slippery blended with shards of crusty meringue, which seemed to melt and disappear on contact. In her mind's eye Phoebe saw Pace holding the spoon in his big tanned hand, his eyes glowing at her pleasure, anticipating the delights yet to come, and suddenly everything but their joined breathing seemed to fade away.

The echo of her heartbeat thudding against her ribs pounded like a far-off sea in her ears. The violins sounded strangely removed, so that the melody, and the violinists themselves, seemed to be in another time and place. When his scent grew stronger and soft warm lips traced her temple Phoebe sucked in air but kept her eyes closed. His breath was an inciting furnace on her skin. She swore she heard the blood booming through his veins. She'd never felt this hot before…doubted she ever would again.

Pace's voice was raw. "Do you want more, Phoebe?"

With her heart hammering in her throat, her head light and beginning to spin, she swallowed what remained of the sugar melting on her tongue and nodded.

She waited for the cool spoon to touch her lips again. Instead she felt Pace's hands curl around her waist. Next she knew, she was lifted off her feet. She opened her eyes at the same moment he set her to sit upon the table. A sparkling waterfall of sensation cascaded through her as, locked in the heat of his eyes, she braced herself for what was to come.

His kiss shot a torrent of effervescence through her body, drew feelings of desire from her that only the gods could know about. His palms were on her shoulders, bringing her towards him, and as his hands drew down her arms the straps of her gown were peeled down too.

With her breasts fully exposed to the exhilarating chill of the night she arched towards him, ready to have him drag the rest of the clothes from her body. But then, in a gut-wrenching flash, she remembered their company. The quartet. What if one of them came out?

Pulling back from his mouth, she shimmied her bodice up to cover herself. "Shouldn't we say good-night to our guests first?"

Unconcerned, he smoothed a spiral of loose hair from her face. "I told them to leave five minutes after we moved out here. That's a CD playing."

Phoebe processed the information, then released a commending smile. "You always think ahead, don't you?"

"I wanted a private evening with you," he explained. "You wanted the same."

She filed her fingers up through his hair. It was true. She did want to be alone with him. Wanted to feel his masculine heat merging with hers. Wanted his smouldering kisses again and again. A week without Pace had seemed like two lifetimes.

Surrendering, she coiled an arm around his neck and lifted herself to meet his lips. Her nipples flared with warmth when his hand wove up her outside leg, tugging her gown all the way up before his fingers slid beneath her panties.

His touch travelled inward at the same time as he groaned against her lips, "Wider, Phoebe. Open wider."

She complied, and with his other hand supporting her weight he laid her back upon the table. Her fingers knotting in his hair, she focused on the giddy rhythm of their mouths working together, on how the growing intensity matched the rising flood of desire drenching her body. She wanted these sensations to last and last. The pleasure was so concentrated. So absolute and vital. Just like those first times. Only this time she knew it would be better. Would *continue* to get better. And that made her feel more confident and desirable than anything.

Arched over her, he lifted her hips and ground them against his. When she tore the shirt tails from his trousers he grasped her panties and ripped them off. A fire, furious and all-consuming, whipped through her blood as Pace unzipped, hastily protected himself, then entered her in one urgent, solid stroke.

Throwing back her head, she gasped and clenched every muscle. He filled her so completely, and yet on the end of the terrific jolt she smiled. She knew from experience there was so much more to come.

His palms cupping her head, he peered into her eyes and began to move. Giving herself over to the drugging magic, she wound her legs around his hips, and as her hands pressed up his slick sides the friction grew brighter and hotter inside. When heat flashed, catching and flying through her veins like a late-summer bushfire, he only thrust deeper—until finally his body locked above hers and her core compressed around a violent whirl of beautiful, burning sensation.

When flaming red turned white-hot, everything but feeling—everything but the need to celebrate and let go—was consumed by searing heat, as well as a feeling—an emotion—Phoebe couldn't afford to dwell on.

It felt so good she never wanted it to end.

Lying in the penthouse's sumptuous bed hours later, Phoebe gazed at the ceiling, still floating, one forearm resting on her brow.

After their conflagration out on the balcony, Pace had swept her up and carried her inside to this magnificent bedroom, which boasted the softest satin quilt and an array of gilded mirrors. He'd slipped her gown down the rest of the way. Then he'd laid her here, upon the finest silk threads, and kissed and stroked her the rest of the way down from her incredible high.

When they'd made love again, although less furiously the second time, their passion had seemed even more intense—as if tonight they'd found an enchanted key that had unlocked every one of the wonders they could share.

Now they lay together in the early dawn, naked, sated, limbs loosely twined. But Phoebe still felt his mouth on her skin…his lips trailing her flesh, his tongue swirling and flicking, his expert touch stirring her desire to a point where she whimpered as he flung her over that soaring, dizzy peak.

She couldn't regret that she'd decided to reply to his invitation, to allow herself this freedom and this sizzling joy again. Last night had been worth any price. She felt good about herself in a way she never had before. And that was a curious state to be in. If she felt so good because of a man, if she could barely see straight for the way he made her feel, didn't that beg the question…?

Mustn't her mother have felt this way about her father? As if she were somehow a *part* of him? That in some inexplicable way they were one?

Phoebe didn't condone the fact that her mother had chased after a man who had not only been no longer interested, but who hadn't wanted to know about the child he'd helped create. But she understood better what it was like to be a woman who'd found the one person who made them feel…*complete*.

That was how she felt with Pace.

Her chest aching, she burrowed into Pace's chest until his arm drew her in. Did she really have to go into work today? Did he? How much time did they have before checkout?

"You okay?" he asked.

She wove her fingers up through the hair on his hard chest. "Just wondering how long we have left here."

"As long as we want."

She smiled to herself. She was hardly a woman of the world, but she had a good idea about how much this place would dent a credit card balance.

"I don't want you to have to pay for two nights. The roses alone…" She sighed, remembering their perfume and rich ruby colour. "They were so beautiful—and so many. You must have raided every florist in town."

His lips nuzzled her hair. "I said before—cost doesn't matter."

"But suites like this—with a quartet and a banquet and imported champagne… It must've cost as much as a weekend in Paris."

He growled playfully at her ear. "I get fringe benefits with my job."

There was nothing *fringe* about this.

A horrible idea gripped her. "I'd hate to think that you'd borrowed money—"

He rolled over and drilled her eyes. "Phoebe, quit worrying. I have enough money to do as I please."

Feeling strangely off balance, she studied his eyes. Not only did he mean what he said, with that statement he'd put an end to her questions.

Enough money to do as he pleased? Well, he drove the best, ate the best, and it seemed wanted to experience the best. And his financial status was none of her business. She ought to simply take his word that he could afford this kind of luxury. It wasn't as if they were planning to pay off a mortgage together.

He lay down again and pressed his lips to her crown. "We'll see each other again tonight?" he said against her hair.

She held her breath, then snuggled closer to his scent and his heat. She wouldn't let doubts interfere this time. She'd come here to relive what they'd enjoyed a week ago. She'd hold on to that…and for as long as she could.

"What do you suggest?" she asked.

"For one, next time I call, you pick up."

When he squeezed her, she laughed softly. "I promise to make myself available."

She watched the lifting shadows of the coming day, wondering if he'd say more or finally fall asleep. Not that she expected to hear anything as monumental as, *I love you…you've changed my world.* That kind of talk was for the movies. In fact she didn't expect anything more than his smouldering attentions.

Last night had made her realise that she was more like her mother than she'd ever have admitted, but that didn't mean she was prepared to have history repeat itself. She wouldn't make a fool of herself over a man. The day she *did* expect more from her relationship with Pace than was wise—the day she felt herself slipping in too deep—was the day it ended and she walked away.

CHAPTER TEN

THEY saw each other every night that week, and as each day passed Phoebe looked more and more forward to seeing Pace again.

Each night at around eleven he dropped her off at her apartment—but he didn't come in, no matter how many times she asked. Maybe he didn't want to tread on Hannie's toes, but dog and date had been getting along by the end of the Tyler's Stream trip. She was certain Hannie would behave if Pace were to visit again.

So when Pace had collected her this time, she'd made a point of saying that Hannie was staying with her neighbour. She didn't want to think about how she would feel if, knowing that, Pace still didn't come in tonight.

They were electric together in the bedroom. So what was the story? Didn't he want to be with her—sleep with her again?

Tonight she chose the restaurant, an authentic Chinese place in The Rocks, with tapestries of the Great Wall and a sweet hostess who wore green beads and couldn't stop smiling. After a wonderful meal, they strolled arm in arm down the Sydney streets and windowshopped.

There were so many jewellery stores, all with spectacular diamond rings winking out at her from plump white satin cushions behind the glass. She'd never had any reason to ogle diamond rings before, other than out of normal female curiosity. But, strolling down the busy lamplit footpath, she couldn't tamp down the tiny thrill running through her as her gaze lingered and her imagination tripped out.

"Something I can help you with there?"

Feeling guilty, Phoebe looked at Pace. "Help? What do you mean?"

"I know about women and jewellery. You mentioned your birthday's coming up. Should we choose something together, or would you rather a surprise?"

He thought she was hinting? Had her fascination with the windows been that obvious?

Smiling, embarrassed, she shook her head. "You don't have to get me anything."

"Of course I do. I want to. Something to go with your eyes." He curled hair behind her ear. "Jade or emerald drops, perhaps. No. You're a diamond girl, aren't you?"

She sighed. "That's not fair." Show her a girl who wasn't.

A hot fingertip drew around her neckline. His lidded gaze followed the movement. Immediately her breasts burned for his touch to drop lower. After almost a week she still craved the feel of his palm pressed against her flesh. The heat of his body slung over hers.

"A necklace," he concluded, collecting her hand and brushing his lips over her inside wrist. "Or a bracelet."

He twirled her so that her back was to his front.

His arms wound around her waist and his cheek rested close to hers. All those jewels in the window glittered out at them—one in particular. A beautiful solitaire, not so much large as dazzling. A thousand prisms of light shot from its centre. The beauty of its brilliance touched something in her heart. Made her eyes a little misty.

Which meant she needed to take a giant step back. He'd asked her about a birthday gift, not getting engaged. Yes, he treated her beautifully. Was attentive and fun and the perfect lover. But in real time she barely knew him, and Pace was only ever supposed to be Mr Right Now. This affair wasn't meant to last.

Was it?

She gripped his forearm holding her waist and surrendered to an overwhelming surge of longing. She was so fiercely attracted to this man, and yet what did she really know about him other than he worked for Brodricks and he had an extravagant nature? They ate at the finest restaurants. Drank the most expensive wines. What must they pay him?

When he nuzzled her neck, uncaring of the curious looks and smiles of passers-by, she held onto the moment, then asked, "How long have you been with Brodricks?"

"Seems like I've always been there."

"So it was your first job?"

"Pretty much."

"They must pay well."

"Pay well?" The breeze coming in from the harbour picked up as he manoeuvred her around to face him. A playful glint sparkled in his eyes. "Are you sure you're a television host, because you'd make a great cross-examiner."

She would have said sorry for prying, but she was only getting to know him better. She wasn't a gold-digger, if that was what he was thinking. She had her own career. A well-paying one.

"I have connections with Brodricks that go way back," Pace conceded, walking again, his arm linked through hers.

"Guess you hope to be promoted higher up the ladder some day?"

"Maybe. Maybe not." His brow creased and his gaze grew distant. "What I'd really like is to head a new development programme. Start from scratch—build something that could wear the Brodricks badge with pride."

"You'd get a big bonus from your boss for that."

His grin was lopsided. "You think? Frankly I can't see him ever releasing the funds." He shrugged. "Maybe best."

They arrived at his car—tonight a cherry-red Ferrari. "Could you top something like this?"

He swung open her door. "Even Enzo had to start somewhere."

It was past eleven. Work tomorrow for them both, and she'd had little sleep the night before. When he dropped her off tonight and she invited him in would he accept? She wanted his arms around her all night. Wanted his scent on her pillow. His smile in the morning. Was he waiting for her to say please?

They drove for a while, and when he turned into a private address elegant automatic gates fanned open. Drowsy from the vibration of the engine, Phoebe realised they were nowhere near her neighbourhood. Only the rich and or seriously famous lived here.

Sitting straighter, she peered out of the window as security lights blinked on over a lawn and gardens which were vast and professionally manicured. The house—it was more a mansion—was Mediterranean in style, two-storey, with heavy timber shutters and doors.

She swept away the hair fallen over her eyes and blinked. "I don't understand."

"I thought it was high time I invited you back to my place," he said, and she couldn't contain a laugh. This wasn't someone's place—it was a palace!

But then she examined his candid face and sobered. "My God. You're serious. This is *your* house?"

"It used to belong to my parents, but, yes, it's mine now. My father designed it, inspired by my mother's Latin ancestry. Spanish splendour at its finest. I bought out my brother's half when our father died."

Phoebe held her freefalling stomach. This had to be some kind of joke. And yet now things were beginning to make sense. He might work for Brodricks, but surely this piece of real estate made him independently wealthy. What other assets did he own?

To one side was an Olympic-sized swimming pool, and change facilities big enough to house a small family. Was that a massive orchard towards the back? She couldn't count the number of garages that graced one side of the property.

Holding her throat, she blew out a shaky breath. "Did you eat caviar when you were a kid?"

"Not for breakfast."

The gates closed behind them and he swung the car

around a spectacular circular drive, the centrepiece of which was an elaborate water feature of a warrior in a chariot, dramatically lit from beneath the pool's surface.

He killed the engine and leaned towards her, his gaze intent, his lips devastatingly inviting.

"Phoebe," he murmured close, "stay the night."

Her head began to swim. She felt as if she were being swept away on a colossal wave, not knowing which direction was up, unable to get enough air. Stay the night? *Here* in this incredible dream of a house that Pace *owned*? Was this real?

"Phoebe?"

She held her brow. She felt so out of her depth. This was a whole other step…an invitation to cross another boundary of his life. Was that a good or a bad thing? It was wonderful to know that he wanted to be with her as much as she wanted to be with him. But was she wanting more—*feeling* more—than was safe?

Her stomach swooped.

Yes.

No.

If she was feeling so confused, she didn't have to do anything tonight. Best she took some time to sort out her emotions—sort out her head—and make a plan of how best to go forward.

She needed an excuse, and quickly—before she changed her mind and followed him like a lamb inside.

"Hannie…he's by himself at home."

"You said he was with your neighbour tonight."

His lips whispered over hers and she said, less

convincingly, "I promised I'd meet Roz early for a coffee."

"Phoebe." His mouth grazed hers, then lingered, rubbing up and down as his lidded eyes smiled in the shadows and his musky scent warmed her blood. "What are you afraid of? It's just a house."

She tried to shift the thickness from her throat. "If you want to know…I'm feeling a little overwhelmed." *About so many things.* "I mean, I want to stay, of course. I'm just having a hard time believing…" Again she drank in her glamorous surrounds. *"All this."*

What came next? Anything? Nothing?

She said, half seriously, "I'm not on a hidden camera reality show, am I?" Then she searched his eyes. "You're not playing some game with me—are you, Pace?"

His hand curled around her nape. Before kissing her again, this time deeply, he said, "No, Phoebe. I'm not playing."

After he released her lips, he let her out of the car and ushered her up the tiled steps that led to the double front doors. Once inside, he didn't give her a tour. In her dazed state, she doubted she would have taken too much in. Even in the muted light, the glittering entry and sweeping staircase was enough to leave her speechless.

A step ahead, he carefully drew her up the stairs and into a room that was as large as her apartment, with a bed as big as her kitchen. With moonlight streaming in through a giant arched window he stopped at the foot of a midnight blue duvet, slid one strap from her shoulder, then the other. His chest expanded a moment, before his hands skimmed down her waist and he dropped a soft, sensual line of kisses around her collarbone. When his tongue trailed her jaw, her chin automatically tipped up. She was trembling so badly with want she wasn't sure her legs would hold out.

His voice was a low, persuasive murmur at her ear. "Stay the night."

When his mouth covered hers she dissolved against him, and her hands drove up against the warm fabric covering his chest. There was no need to reply. He knew her answer.

She couldn't say no if she tried.

CHAPTER ELEVEN

Two weeks later, Pace swung his red Ducati 916 into Brodricks and parked beside Nick's Audi. Nick detested motorbikes. He didn't like the look of them. Didn't like their sound.

Grinning, Pace revved a couple more times, then wound the throaty engine down. Nothing like setting the tone for the day. Although these past weeks he hadn't been quite so ticked off by Nick and his strutting around the place, trying to impress.

His smile slipping, Pace removed his helmet and swung his leg over and onto the ground.

Eldest son made good. And now that Nick was at the top there'd be no getting him down. Not that Pace wanted that job back. No way. Absolutely not.

But lately he had been thinking about his alias… about whether it had outgrown its usefulness. He couldn't live under another name all his life, although he was certain Nick wouldn't object; he was happiest when Pace Davis walked a step behind him.

Moving towards the main building, Pace cast a look around the grounds. Men were busy erecting a giant marquee and amenities for tonight's annual client and sponsor cocktail party. Once, not so long ago, Pace wouldn't have missed that kind of event. He'd liked the music, the conversation. Most of all he'd liked the surplus of interesting female company. But he wouldn't be making an appearance tonight. Phoebe was coming over, as she'd done every night these past weeks. They would have their own conversation.

Make their own music.

In jeans and a white dress shirt, no tie, Pace strode into the main entrance, where a football field's worth of high-powered motoring luxury gleamed in the morning light. Nodding at Lance, their regular cleaner, then looking towards the offices, Pace felt his senses tingle and he slowed up. Was it imagination or had Nick kept a lower profile of late?

Pace had to grin. Maybe his brother was busy preparing his hour-long speech for tonight?

But Nick *had* seemed less in his face—maybe because of his preoccupation with Phoebe and the sensational way she made him feel. Strong and confident. But more so. Happy with himself and the world in a way he'd never experienced—not even when he'd earned his driver's licence or accepted his degree in cap and gown. Whenever he and Phoebe were together his mind and body interacted in a predictable way and in an instant he was ready to take her in his arms and make love until they were both spent. He couldn't get enough of the silky warmth of her body, *sans* clothes, curled up around him at night. But was that all he wanted from her?

"You okay, Pace? You look like you forgot something."

His mind snapping back, Pace found Lance, chamois in hand, standing close by, studying him.

Smiling, he shifted his helmet to his other hand and ran some fingers through his hair. "I'm fine. A bit distracted, is all."

Truth was, he'd been distracted by Phoebe since the night they'd met. And the fascination kept growing. Any time they were together a powerhouse of energy simmered and sparked. Having dinner, watching a movie, going for a drive, she affected him. To his core. And when they joined together in the bedroom that powerhouse caught light and exploded, again and again.

She was like no other woman he'd known. He couldn't get enough of her. This morning when she'd kissed him goodbye, humming against his lips while the tips of her breasts had trailed over his chest, he'd struggled not to drag her back under the covers and ask her. No more wasting time going back and forth. This weekend he was going to ask her to move in.

Drastic measures.

But an irresistible temptation.

Although another question had niggled these past days, too.

How would she take it when he explained there was more to Pace Davis—aka Davis Pace Brodrick? A lot more. Like being tossed out of the top job in disgrace three years ago because he'd been too busy having a good time. Would she tell him that life could be complicated and that she understood why he'd kept it from her? More likely she'd be hurt. But no one blurted out their history, warts and all, on the first or second date. Even the third or fourth. At least *he* didn't.

Although there *had* been a lot of getting-to-know-everything-about-each-other talk on her side.

When *was* the time to come clean?

Pace tipped his head in greeting at Derrick Wilson as they passed in the corridor. Derrick's face looked lined, his glasses a little askew. No wonder. Pace shuddered. Who'd want to be an accountant?

As he neared the main wing Pace imagined Brodricks' president slaving away, as usual, at his desk, poring over figures, crossing all his "t"s. But when he strolled by the office door his step faltered.

Sitting behind his desk, head in hands, Nick looked ready to reach for the nearest noose. His usually immaculately styled dark hair was mussed. The knot of his tie hung halfway down his shirt.

Pace scrubbed his jaw. What was going on? Had something happened to Amy?

When the pager on Pace's belt sounded, Nick dragged his bloodshot gaze up from his blotter. Without discerning the caller, Pace disarmed the message and entered the massive oak and leather office.

Nick's gaze fell to his desk again, but not in his usual self-important way. There were circles under his eyes. His face was unshaven. Pace sensed he barely had energy to speak.

"Doesn't look like a very good morning," Pace observed.

"That would be correct."

Nick's speech was thick and slurred. Was he smashed at eight in the morning? But his brother barely drank. Pace's gaze swept the room. No empty Scotch glasses. No crushed beer cans.

Pace took in the plaques on the wall, the Italian crafted furniture and the million-dollar coffee machine gleaming in one corner. Hundreds of clients had been entertained in this room, all eager to sign on the dotted line and spend exorbitant amounts on a luxury vehicle or two. This morning Nick barely looked capable of lifting a pen.

Pace edged closer. "Everything okay at home?"

His brother didn't respond. Didn't move.

Nick was never anything other than on top, or fighting tooth and nail to get there. This lethargic, almost shattered man had Pace wondering if he'd stepped into the twilight zone. Where was the parry and thrust? The digs and wise-ass cracks.

Pace began to ask again, but Nick interrupted with a curt, "At home, Pace, everything is just great."

"Are you sick?"

Sitting back, Nick picked up the phone, punched in a key. "I have a meeting in an hour, and—"

"And you can cancel—" Pace crossed the room and now swiped the receiver from his brother's hand "—until you tell me what on earth is going on. If this has nothing to do with Amy, it's about business. The business that's still fifty percent mine."

Whatever was amiss, Pace wanted to know. Dammit, he *deserved* to know. And not next week. *Now.*

Nick glared at him, his dark brown eyes rimmed with red. "If you recall, it was deemed best that the running of this company be left to *me*."

Pace's temper snapped. He slammed his helmet on the desk and swung Nick's chair towards him. Gripping the armrests, he bent close and lowered his voice. "Nick, your hands are shaking, for God's sake. Crazy idea, but you never know. Maybe I can help."

Nick blinked, and held his brother's gaze for several moments before the tension leaked from his body and he slid his tie from around his neck the rest of the way.

"Suppose you're going to find out anyway," he drawled. "Might as well get it over with."

A stone sank in Pace's stomach. He recognised the look in his brother's eyes. Defeat. Stung pride. The same feelings Pace had struggled with three years ago, when he'd had that massive blowout and had to step down from the chair. On that day Pace hadn't wanted to look Nick, or anyone else, in the eye. Nick hadn't made it easy for him—then or any time after. Not that Pace had expected him to. That was how their relationship had been defined. Locked horns all the way.

And yet now…

His chest tight, Pace pulled out a chair, sat down, and spoke without anger or accusation.

"Nick…let me help."

Nick's nostrils flared. He drilled Pace's gaze, his eyes stormy. But Pace didn't react. He loved this place as much as his brother did. He needed to know what the problem was, and being a jerk wouldn't help.

Hell, it never had.

Gradually the venom in Nick's eyes faded, until all that remained was a bleak glare of desolation.

Nick's Adam's apple bobbed twice. "I'm in trouble," he ground out. "Big trouble."

For the next hour Pace listened to how Nick had wanted do their father's memory proud and excel in all areas of the president's position. He wanted Brodricks to grow and do more. *Be* more. Two years ago Nick had kicked off negotiations with a group of engineers outside of the company, people who were known as brilliant but extreme in their perceptions regarding automobiles of tomorrow. They and Nick had discussed, in depth, the possibility of creating a supercar which would carry the Brodricks badge.

Pace was floored. He and Nick had been rivals, certainly, but with his knowledge and experience he should have been consulted. It made bad business sense *not* to.

"Why didn't you talk to me?"

"Pride," Nick admitted. "Stupidity. You'd talked about doing the same thing. From a purely business angle, I knew we ought to sit down. From a personal stand...I didn't want you to steal any of my thunder."

Nick went on to explain how he'd poured money into the project—initially his own, and then the company's. But each new technology or material they'd hoped to incorporate into the plan had never quite been ready. But would be soon. Always soon.

"I put more funds in, and more. Last night the man I've been communicating with rang and said they'd suffered a setback and would need at least another two years. I told them our cashflow didn't have two years."

Nick closed his eyes, and Pace cringed at the sick feeling his brother must be enduring. No doubt had been enduring since that phone call last night.

Groaning, Nick dragged open his eyes. "I screwed up."

Yeah. But...

Pace rolled back his shoulders. "We all screw up."

Nick looked at him sideways. "I don't get it. This is your chance. Why aren't you grinding your heel into my back?"

"Because the company won't survive if we both keep

behaving like kids. And, frankly, I'm over it, Nick—aren't you?"

Nick held his brother's gaze for an interminable time, then nodded slowly.

When Pace grinned, Nick smiled and nodded again, more firmly this time. They held out their hands and shook—a first. And it felt good. After all this time, as grown men, it felt right.

Some colour back in his gills, Nick reached for the muscle ball he kept on his desk and squeezed. His brother said it helped him think.

"So…" Nick sat forward. "What do we do?"

"Something radical. Something never heard of before." Pace pushed to his feet. "We work together. Starting now."

Early that evening, Phoebe pulled into Pace's house-cum-mansion and steered her gorgeous BMW up the wide pine-lined drive.

What would they do tonight? Not *later* tonight. She knew precisely how *that* part of the evening would play out, and where they would end up—in bed, spiralling and reaching for the stars together. She'd thought that after a few times of physically being together the thrill might settle into something more ordinary. But the sensations had gone the other way. *Higher.* And they were still climbing, becoming more concentrated and vital each and every time they made love.

Sometimes when Pace brought her to climax—using the skill of his hands or his mouth or the heavenly old-fashioned way—she wasn't able to catch her breath. At those moments she swore she wouldn't care if she expired entirely, she felt so sublimely whole...prized and cared for.

Leaving him in the mornings was hard, even when she knew she'd be back that night. During the day Pace would always call to ask about her plans and tell her to come over straight after work. She longed to tease and say no even once, to see what he'd say. But she couldn't bring herself to do anything other than agree, and then count down the minutes until they saw each other again.

When morning came it was the same deal. Drive home. Drive to work. Wait for his call.

Unbuckling her belt, sliding out from the seat, Phoebe swept aside the quiver of unease she'd felt these past hours. Today had been different. He hadn't phoned, and she hadn't been able to get in touch with him. She wasn't concerned. Not really. Before she'd left this morning he'd called her sweetheart and murmured seductively against her lips, "See you tonight."

Of course this affair was supposed to have been temporary—what she'd needed more than anything at the time. She had vowed that she wouldn't allow herself to feel more for smooth-talking Pace Davis than was safe.

But they were so good together, she reasoned, making her way up to the porch. Light years beyond good.

Finding a smile, she leapt up the front steps.

Now that they knew each other, she felt safer with Pace than she had felt in her life. She couldn't imagine a time when these blissful nights would end. She wanted her life to go on and on just as it did now. Even Steve's jibes at work couldn't bother her. Of course it didn't hurt that the ratings for her show had gone through the roof. When you were this happy, each day seemed to feed off the previous one and the whole world was naturally brighter.

When she hadn't heard from Pace, she'd decided to go home to shower and pick out an extra-special outfit to wear. Now, after smoothing her designer yellow silk sheath, she siphoned down a breath and rang the sombre bell—once and twice. She waited several moments—longer than was usual—and was about to ring again when Pace swung open the heavy door.

When his eyes locked with hers, his expression was taken aback, and the smile slid from her face like ice off a plate. Then he smacked his forehead and cursed under his breath.

Her stomach clenched and a massive lump formed in her throat.

He'd *forgotten*? That wasn't possible. He'd seemed so keen this morning. As keen as she'd been. But his reaction and attire said he had other plans. No one wore a tuxedo around the house.

Swallowing against the lump, Phoebe tacked up the heavy corners of her mouth. "We're still on for tonight, right?"

He snatched a kiss from her cheek, then absently checked his gold cufflinks. "Something's come up. Something I can't get out of. I, uh…" He checked his links again. "I have to work late tonight at Brodricks."

Her brows lifted. "You have to work late in a dinner suit?"

He caught the time on his watch and squared shoulders that looked all the more magnificent in that perfectly fitting dinner jacket. "I'm sorry, but I don't have time right now." He threw a look back over his shoulder. "You can stay if you want."

Her heart dropped.

If you want?

She recovered as quickly as she could from the *thunk*. "No, no, I'm good," she said. If she were being dismissed, she wasn't about to sit around, chomping on her nails, wondering when his car would rumble up the drive. She'd go crazy.

Her throat backed up with sudden tears, she shrugged. What was there left to say?

"Guess I'll see you later."

"You mean tomorrow?" He tugged an ear, thinking, then announced, "That might be best." He held her shoulders and searched her eyes with a determination that rekindled some of her hope. "I can't get out of this."

From the lounge room, a phone rang out. He turned on his heel to catch it, then, as an afterthought, swung back to drop another kiss on her cheek. He squeezed her arm. "I'll call."

A moment later Phoebe was walking back to her car on rubbery legs, alone and dazed. The same words kept swirling through her mind. *What had just happened?* Her more rational side told her to chill. Pace had an important business engagement that he'd forgotten about. Simple.

But he'd also forgotten to call her today. Had forgotten she was coming over tonight. Normally he would seduce her with his eyes the moment they saw each other again. The intent had always rippled off him in hot, shimmering waves, drawing her in, making her melt.

Not so long ago it had seemed she couldn't get rid of him.

A disturbing thought crept into the curling edges of her mind. Biting a thumbnail, she cast a questioning look back over her shoulder.

Was he really working late? Or did he have another less professional appointment to rush off to?

She slid inside her car, moisture filling her eyes and raw emotion choking off her air. Wringing her hands on the steering wheel, she breathed all the way in, then out, while telling her thumping heartbeat to quieten. She'd never felt more devastated in her life. Which was over the top.

Nevertheless, wanting to curl up into a ball, she groaned.

Oh, God, she wasn't thinking straight. This minute the most logical plan she could come up with was knocking on his door again and asking if he still cared for her. Of course he did. He *must*.

But how much? Clearly not as much as she cared for him. He wasn't sitting somewhere shaking, wondering if this was the beginning of the end.

Forcing herself to get a grip, she sat taller.

Okay. Obvious call. This was the time to bow out. She was feeling way too much, way too deeply. She'd wondered if the fireworks might weaken after they'd been together a few times. She hated to think about it, but...

Maybe they had for him.

Pace stood inside the glass enclosure, unseen by the black tie crowd milling outside the Brodricks building. A ball of nerves rolled around in his stomach. Soon he'd be out there, addressing business associates, industry gurus and clients. A second chance.

And his brother would be standing beside him.

Pace swung his jacket off the rack and thrust his arms through the sleeves.

He and Nick were both determined to make this work. Pace had verbally committed his private resources to help haul Brodricks out of its current hole. And once the brothers had sat down with Derrick Wilson and discussed the options calmly the prognosis hadn't looked quite as dim. Reshaping was needed, and a cutback in stock, as well as a general tightening of belts. But it was doable.

None of that meant he—or Nick for that matter—needed to give up on plans to pioneer a luxury car which some day would proudly bear the Brodricks badge. Still, any further plans in that direction would kick off only after they were soundly back on their feet, and they'd do it as a team.

Fidgeting with his tie, Pace found a grin.

With Nick on his side, and vice versa, Pace was more than ready to do this job right. He'd never thought this day would come, but now it was here he was almost grateful that the company had hit this pothole. God knew how much longer he and Nick would have clung onto past grievances if not for this glitch. Now, rather than competing, they were committed to working together.

As brothers should.

After running a hand down his satin lapels, taking in one last settling breath, Pace fanned back the door. When the bustle of the crowd and the music hit him, he remembered where he'd been the same time last night…in his bedroom, with the woman who was as insatiable for him as he was for her.

He'd felt like mud when Phoebe had knocked on his door earlier. She'd looked so gutted. But he hadn't forgotten her…not completely. He'd remembered during the day to call, but had postponed when he'd become distracted again with Nick and Derrick Wilson. His mind had been ticking over so fast when he'd got home…

Setting off, Pace shouldered his way through the crowd.

None of that was an excuse for breaking their date. Neither did he have a choice. Things had changed. Changed dramatically. He'd get tonight out of the way—discussions with Nick were bound to leach into the early hours—and he would call Phoebe in the morning. By this time tomorrow everything would be out in the open and they could resume where they left off.

If she didn't hate him for keeping the truth behind his identity under wraps, and *if* she could accept he wouldn't have nearly as much time as he'd used to.

He'd been too easily distracted five years ago, the first time round. Now he was determined to put his all into succeeding—just as his father had. Brodricks and Nick needed him as much as he needed them. No more slacking off. No more bickering. Nose to the grindstone two hundred percent. Making this place strong again—redeeming himself—was his number one priority.

This time nothing would stand in his way.

CHAPTER TWELVE

AFTER an hour driving aimlessly around, Phoebe came to a decision—one she didn't feel wholly right about but was committed to nonetheless.

Now, as she swerved the BMW into Brodricks, her tummy somersaulted. The car park was packed, filled with every kind of luxury car, many with uniformed drivers perched, waiting, behind their wheels. Subtle strains of music lilted in the background. Colourful arcs from strobe lights—purple, yellow and blue—fanned from a giant marquee erected beyond the extensive Brodricks building.

Easing out from the car cabin, Phoebe rubbed her damp palms together. She'd come to see if Pace were here. Whether he was indeed working late. She hadn't expected this spectacle.

But now it made sense. Pace had said he needed to work late at Brodricks. A black tie function. The boss had probably flung him a "must attend" ticket late this afternoon. Maybe he had to make some sort of speech or presentation. That was why he'd seemed hassled.

A chilly pre-winter breeze ruffled her knee-length hem and her toes curled in their strappy heels. Now she knew he had a legitimate reason for his attire and behaviour this evening she wondered if she should get back in her car, give him his space and wait for his call. She didn't want him to think she was spying. Even though she was.

And, heck, now she was here...

Maybe when this affair was over they could do something together. Get back to that good place where they both liked to be. Where nothing mattered but being together.

Another breeze stirred around her feet. Hugging herself against the cool, she hurried towards a twinkling arbour where a young uniformed man extended his hand in friendly greeting.

"Brodricks is pleased you could join us..."

As the man went on, Phoebe held up a hand. She wasn't a guest. Not exactly.

"I'm with Pace Davis." The man's brows jumped. Apparently he needed more information. "Pace is Chief Technical Adviser here."

The man checked his list and, satisfied, ushered her through. Amid the crush of evening gowns and suits, an eager waiter fell upon her.

"Care for refreshment, ma'am?"

She shook her head. "But could you tell me where I could find Pace Davis? He's wearing a tuxedo—" She glanced around and blushed. "Right. Of course. Everyone is. But he's very tall, with very dark hair and—"

At that moment the music died and all heads swung towards a striking-looking man who waited behind a microphone on the stage.

"Good evening, everyone," the man at the microphone said. "Thank you for coming to what I know will be a special evening for us all. I'm Nicholas Brodrick—"

The waiter leaned towards Phoebe and whispered, "He's the boss."

Phoebe nodded, unable to do anything other than follow the crowd's lead and focus on the spokesperson; she knew his name from the sponsorship agreement.

As Nicholas Brodrick talked on about interesting new directions and challenging economic times, for some strange reason she felt they'd met. His face… something in his expression…seemed familiar.

She shrugged the prickling feeling off.

Most likely she'd bumped into him the other week when she'd come to collect her car. Still, his smile— subtle yet compelling—she felt almost close to.

"This is a very special and interesting time," he was saying, "not only from a business perspective but also a personal one. I've been President of Brodricks these past three years. Tonight I'd like to welcome my new co-president to the stage. It's my honour to welcome back to the top chair someone who knows this business inside and out."

On tiptoe, Phoebe scanned the sea of unfamiliar faces. This news was likely interesting to others here, but she only wanted to track down Pace. Maybe a better idea would be to surprise him and be there waiting when he showed up at his place later. Surely this event wouldn't go past midnight? She was used to staying up with Pace much later than that.

Nick Brodrick continued. "Some of you will be fa-miliar with him. Until today he was our Chief Mechanic and Technical Adviser—"

Phoebe's ears pricked.

Technical Adviser? This man was introducing *Pace*?

"Please make welcome," the man elaborated, "the new co-president of Brodricks Prestige Cars...my brother...Davis Brodrick!" The man raised his hands in welcome and everyone applauded. Everyone—

—except Phoebe.

Her hands were poised and ready, but her expression dropped. Perhaps she hadn't heard correctly. She didn't understand. Words seemed to be messed up in her brain. Had that man said Davis Brodrick? But *Pace* was the Chief Technical Adviser here.

Amidst the stir, Phoebe caught a glimpse of a tall, athletically built man cleaving his way through the crowd with the force of a mighty god parting the sea. With lights beating and music blaring a fanfare, the cacophony continued to usher the man of the moment in. When Phoebe caught a good look at the face—the coal-black hair, those electric blue eyes...

The strength left her body. She felt king-hit. Remembering how he'd chased her, how he'd said he wasn't playing, how he might as well have pushed her out through the door tonight...

Her vision tunnelled and her knees gave way.

The waiter managed his tray with one hand while catching her with the other as she slid towards the ground. His glasses rattling, he rasped, "Lady, are you all right?"

Her surroundings pulled in and out. Colours faded; sounds too. The applause regressed into a muffled din that fogged her mind while faces faded out. Everyone— *everything*—seemed to be laughing at her.

The man on stage—*Pace's brother?*—spoke again.

"Davis Brodrick, ladies and gentlemen."

Phoebe found her balance and forced her mind to work.

Pace was related to the Brodricks? The family who'd acquired a fortune over the last two decades via their prestige automobile links?

She closed her eyes and her fingers began to tingle.

He'd slept with her—so many times—but he hadn't bothered to mention his real name. Had he ever planned to tell her? Was she the only one on the planet who *hadn't* known?

She held her cheeks as her face began to burn.

She'd thought she had it so together. She was nothing but a first-class fool.

The noise of the party filtered through the haze. Gathering herself, only knowing that she needed to escape, she headed for the exit at the same time as Pace's gaze caught hers. Through the animated crowd she saw his face darken, his square jaw clench, and the burning anxiety condensing in her stomach shot up the back of her throat.

Whether he'd seen her or not, she expected him to continue on to the stage. She prayed that he would. She couldn't face him. Her mind was whirling so much she wouldn't know what to say, what to do.

When his paused step detoured and arrowed straight for her Phoebe's palms began to sweat. Then he was standing in front of her while intrigued spectators paused in their applause to suss out this new twist.

While Phoebe stood frozen—*crushed*—Pace flung a black look around at the entranced audience and, catching her elbow, steered her off to a quiet spot away from the glares.

The murmuring grew, and then she heard Nick Brodrick apologise into the microphone, asking for everyone's patience. Pace set his hands on the brick wall either side of her head and drilled her eyes like a provoked warden.

"What are you doing here?"

Phoebe couldn't block the inappropriate urge to laugh. This was so bizarre. Maybe there was a cup of tea she could drink that would make everything in upside-down-land go right side up again.

She held her brow, the remains of a stunned smile stamped on her face.

He wanted to know what *she* was doing here?

She shook her head. "I—I don't really know." She'd come to check up on him, then to wait for him. Now... "All I know is...I need to go."

Pressing a palm to her churning stomach, she ducked to leave, but he herded her back in.

"I was going to explain," he said.

She swallowed against the rock wedged high in her throat. "Then me coming here saved you time."

"I didn't lie to you. I *am* Pace Davis." His brow creased. "It was a business decision made years ago."

She followed her own logic. "And I was *business*?"

His mouth tightened. "It's a long, complicated story."

"We all have one of those. I didn't keep mine from you."

And her past would have been a whole lot harder to talk about than admitting that you were some filthy rich hotshot who for some reason wanted to hide behind another name. Her body, her heart, felt so heavy. She'd never felt more betrayed.

She swallowed against the choking ache in her windpipe. "What's this all about, Pace? Who are you?"

The light reflecting in his eyes flared before he stood back and straightened. He was so tall and broad and masterful she felt dwarfed by his presence.

"I'm the second son of Nicholas Brodrick Senior, founder of Brodricks Prestige Cars. When my father died he bequeathed ownership to both Nick, my brother, and I, but I was to take the president's chair. Nick wasn't happy. And neither was I…completely. The industry side of the business I loved—the engineering aspects, the travel, test-driving and importing the most expensive, coveted automobiles in the world. But I wasn't so keen on immersing myself in the daily grind of figures and endless board meetings. That was Nick's forte."

Pressing her lips together, Phoebe caught a sob. She'd thought she'd known him. She'd known *nothing*. She might as well be looking at a stranger. She'd been sleeping with someone, sharing everything she was, with a man who'd worn a mask.

Her voice cracked. "Why didn't you tell me all this before?"

His fractious look said he was telling her now. "I stepped down from the company's limelight three years ago and Nick stepped up. Today I learned that Brodricks is in trouble again. If it's going to survive, Nick and I need to work together."

Holding her brow, Phoebe tried to take in all the turns. "Why the alias?"

He hesitated a moment, and in the shadows she saw his eyes darken. "When I stepped down from the presidency it was with egg on my face. I needed to dodge the media spotlight. So I put a spin on my name to get them off my heels before I went overseas. The name stuck when I came back."

"And now?"

"Now you know everything."

Not everything. "What does this mean for us?"

"Nothing's changed." His chin came down. "Other than I'll need to spend more time here at work until things settle."

"How long?"

"A year. Two. I don't know." His shrug verged on the impatient. "Does it matter?"

After these past weeks? "It does to me."

"You think a better idea would be to let my father's life's work slide down the toilet while I sit back playing house?"

"Is that what we were doing? Playing house?"

Exasperated, he closed his eyes and held his brow with a curved palm. Finally he dropped his hand and fused her gaze with his.

"There's a crowd of people waiting. I won't argue. Whatever came before, this is who I am. A son and brother who is taking on the biggest challenge of his life and won't quit until it's won." His brow pinched. "Can you understand how important this is to me?"

She nodded carefully. He seemed blinded by it. His every gesture radiated determination. His life had taken an unexpected turn which, it seemed, wasn't unwelcome. He was telling her that not only was his mind made up, but he had other priorities now.

The noise outside seemed to fade up as a head ducked in the alcove—Nick Brodrick, Pace's brother. Or should she call him Davis now?

"Sorry to interrupt," Nick said. "Just wondering…an estimate…when do you think you'll be joining us?"

A muscle in his jaw popped as Pace shoved his hands in his pockets. "I'll be out in a minute."

Nick sent Phoebe a cordial nod. When he left there seemed little else to say. Pace had to go. She had to step back. Hadn't she always suspected this time would come? Everything had pointed to a short, hot love affair. She'd gone into this fully informed.

Didn't mean it hurt any less.

Pace pulled his hands from his pockets, but he held off from reaching for her.

His voice dropped, became consoling. "Look, we're both strung out, and this situation isn't going to ease up for a while. I'll be working long hours, going overseas a lot, and you've got your show that's doing so well."

When he held her eyes, his pupils dilating, Phoebe's chest tightened till she flinched.

"Pace…what are you saying?"

His jaw popped again. "If it's too complicated… maybe we ought to give it a rest for a while."

The world tipped on its axis and Phoebe swayed. She felt as if every drop of blood had been drained from her body. As if every spark of life she'd ever owned had fizzled out. But these past weeks she'd grown so much. She'd found an aspect of herself that had made her that much stronger. For that experience she had Pace to thank. If she had to walk away, at least she'd walk away with that. And if it was time to go, she'd do it gracefully. No drawn-out goodbyes. No dramatics.

Lifting her chin, she managed a no-hard-feelings smile. "Maybe that would be best."

His eyes widened before he cocked his head. "I see." He drew down a breath. Blew it out. "So…I'll call."

Her gaze drank in every angle of his beautiful face. She'd never forget him. Even if her heart were breaking. They'd had such wonderful times together—how could she not wish him well? If he'd changed these past weeks, then so had she.

"I'm happy you're excited about becoming you again," she offered.

The intensity in his eyes lifted a little, and the beginnings of a smile hooked his mouth. "I'm not a whole new person. My bike's not going anywhere."

She smiled back, even while she died a little more inside. "So I'll see you around."

His gaze dropped to her lips. He cupped her cheek and she quivered, waiting for his last kiss. She'd carve the memory into her mind and treasure it for ever.

But his mouth pressed not against her lips but her brow, and although disappointment pulsed through her Phoebe soaked in his scent, absorbed the liberating feel of his touch. When he pulled away—when he *walked* away—an odd calm settled over her.

She'd never been so sure of anything. Whatever name he went by, she loved Pace. She loved him with all her soul. And feared she always would.

CHAPTER THIRTEEN

A WEEK later, Phoebe was still numb.

She'd acted in a mature fashion, accepting the inevitable, and had watched Pace walk away. No good could come from clinging when obviously Pace's passion for her was running out of steam. Still, she was agonisingly aware of how easy it would be to call him, or show up unexpectedly, and explain that she knew it could work—she only needed a little time to get over the fact that she'd been humiliated, knowing that he'd kept his true identity a secret the entire time they'd been together.

In the same situation that was what her mother would've done.

Her mum had been desperately in love and, it seemed, hadn't been able to handle "the end". Phoebe had always resented the fact that her mother hadn't put her child before her need to be with a philanderer—a man who hadn't wanted to know either of them.

While Phoebe still wished her mother hadn't left that rainy night, at least now she could appreciate the passion that had propelled her to go. Once you loved someone, that emotion couldn't be turned off like a switch. The beautiful memories, the ache of loss and longing, were always there. Phoebe couldn't imagine a time when this cruel throb beneath her ribs would ease. Couldn't think of a time when she wouldn't be hopelessly in love with Pace.

She might be stronger than her mother—she had no intention of running after Pace, no matter how much her weaker side begged her to. But perhaps that was because she'd lived her life in the shadow of a tragic consequence brought about by someone who couldn't let go.

Until now Phoebe hadn't acknowledged quite how angry she'd been with her mother; those feelings had always simmered, hidden beneath her surface. She would never stop wishing that her mother were alive, but at last she'd forgiven her. Love, in all its forms, was the most powerful force in the world. It could lift you higher than a rocket ship. Could also fling you down and break you like a glass vase.

Empty. Shattered.

Phoebe didn't want to live like that.

Instead, these past days she'd thrown herself into her work, and had filled her time in the evenings catching up with friends. She'd been so determined to hide her pain, not even her best mate Roz had guessed how torn up she was about "that man with the bike you were seeing".

Walking down the main corridor of Goldmar Studios, her mind stuck on Pace, Phoebe stopped when a deep voice from behind shot over her head.

"Where have you been? Having another three-hour pow-wow in the make-up room?"

Withering inside, Phoebe recognised the voice and, without enthusiasm, turned around. Exuding his usual superior air, her boss stood before her. After no sleep this week, she *so* didn't need this now.

She rubbed a gritty eye. "What do you want, Steve?"

"You've been riding high in the ratings this week."

Her jaw unhinged. *Sorry?* "Was that a compliment?"

"We've decided to add another dimension. Another host to share the spotlight."

If he wanted her to bite, he'd be disappointed. She couldn't be bothered retaliating. He wanted a co-host on the show? Fine. He was the boss.

"Send me the details," she said.

But his mouth shifted in a way that told her he was peeved by her easy acceptance. "There's also the matter of your contract, of course." He held up a copy of, she presumed, said contract. "Now that there'll be two hosts, a renegotiation's necessary to even up the budget."

She took a double-take. "You're telling me the show is doing so well that I have to accept a pay *cut*?"

He rolled his eyes. "I was hoping you wouldn't be difficult."

She felt so beaten, at first she automatically decided to get this over with and agree to whatever. But then the words stuck in the back of her throat. She knew what she ought to say, but she couldn't make herself say them.

She couldn't do this any more. She was a professional, but she was also *over* copping Steve's ill treatment on the chin. Going to the top and complaining was an option. But even if she won against Steve's harassment, frankly, she didn't know that she wanted to be stuck in

this environment any more. Was any job—any*thing*—
worth this angst?

A smug look on his face, Steve was wheeling away,
contract held high. "Be in my office by six."

The steel in her voice came naturally. "I have somewhere to be at six."

She wouldn't be treated like a doormat any more. If
she was strong enough to walk away from the man she
loved, surely she could tell this jerk to jam it.

Steve slowly angled back. The contract crumpled
in his hand when he made fists and set them low on
his belt. "I'll be clear. Be there, or don't come back
tomorrow."

Phoebe's patience levels climbed into the red. Since
breaking up with Steve she hadn't thought she had any
choice other than to ride out his chauvinist trip. But she
did have a choice, and it looked more appealing by the
second.

Her gaze dropping to the contract, she put out her
hand. One corner of his mouth curled up in a satisfied
grin as he handed the papers over. Without preamble,
she flipped to the last page, where a signature was re-
quired. When she wiggled her fingers for a pen, Steve
supplied one gladly. Then she hooked a finger, telling
him *come here*. Suspicion glinting in his eyes, he sized
her up, but then stepped closer. Lifting the contract, she
used his chest as a flat surface upon which to sign.

She felt the heat of his hand hovering near her hip,
remembered how it had felt to have him touch her, and
cringed. Thank God she'd ended it when she had.

"There now," he crooned as she wrote. "That wasn't
so hard, was it?"

"Surprisingly much easier than I thought."

For a punctuation mark, she stabbed the pen into the paper.

Steve jumped back, cursing and holding the pinprick in his shirt. He gaped down. "That *hurt*."

She batted her lashes. "Sorry."

After sending her a death glare, he tracked down her autograph. When his gaze landed on the spot, he blinked rapidly and began to wheeze and hyperventilate. "Wha—what's this?"

"I'll be clear." She slotted the pen in his shirt pocket and, before walking off, enunciated two words.

"I. Quit."

That evening, Pace and Nick sat in the artificial light of the new co-president's office, working on quarterly sales figures and projections for the coming year.

Pace was on edge—but not because he couldn't cope with the rows of numbers; he seemed to have more tolerance for financial statements and economic forecasts these days. He was itchy because he couldn't stop thinking about Phoebe. The way they'd parted. How low he'd felt afterwards.

Before walking away that night he'd said he'd call. He hadn't. The message in Phoebe's glistening eyes couldn't be mistaken. After learning that he'd used an alias the entire time they were together—that he'd hidden so much from her—she didn't want anything more to do with him. Given he hadn't had two minutes spare since, accepting her wishes had seemed kinder to them both. A clean break was a good break.

Not that any part of this break was remotely good.

"You thinking about your girl again?"

Pace glanced up from the latest report Derrick Wilson had put together to meet his brother's concerned gaze.

"She's not my girl, Nick." Tapping his pen against the conference table, he muttered, "Not any more."

"Sorry things didn't work out. You obviously cared a great deal for her."

Pace flinched at the stab beneath his ribs, but quickly shrugged it off. "You know what they say. It was good while it lasted."

Nick nodded. Then, a line forming between the dark slashes of his brows, he scratched his jaw. "From what you told me of your time together, I'm still not clear why you're throwing it away."

Sitting back, Pace growled. "Don't start, Nick." He was in no mood for any brother-to-brother "I know best because I'm older than you" talk.

But Nick held up his hands. "Easy, mate. All I'm saying is that if what you had with Phoebe is even half of what I have with Amy, you'd be an idiot to walk away."

"You're forgetting. Phoebe's the one who let me know she was happy for me to back off." Sure, he'd suggested they take time out. He had a job to do and he couldn't—*wouldn't*—blow it again. But Pace would always remember the nights they'd spent together, how he'd only had to look into her eyes to know she was his. Completely. Unreservedly.

But that was yesterday.

"It's over. I'm head to tail into this." Pace pinched his nose to kill an annoying sting. "Besides, she'd never feel the same way." Or look at him all starry-eyed the way she'd used to.

"She doesn't trust you," Nick concluded.

"Not as far as she can throw a cow."

"Then convince her that she *can*," Nick said, reaching for his coffee cup. "You can do that. I know first-hand. And don't wait until middle age rolls around to do it. There are lots of women in the world, but only one right one." He took a long sip before his cup rattled back into its saucer. "Want some advice?"

Habit had Pace about to say he'd heard enough. But when he saw the sincerity shining in his brother's eyes he relaxed and nodded. "Shoot."

Nick leaned forward. "If you've found the right one, find a way. Make it work. Admit you were wrong to let her go. Bring her back and, most important of all, never let her go again."

CHAPTER FOURTEEN

GOSSIP always shot around the television industry grapevine at lightning speed.

The day after Phoebe had resigned, feeling a little lost but nonetheless pleased that she'd stuck up for herself, she'd taken a call from a rival network. The executive producer there had explained they had a new primetime show launching and they wanted her to host it. When he'd stated their contract terms, Phoebe had stammered and stuttered into the mouthpiece. Did people truly earn that much?

But she hadn't said yes. She'd needed time to get her bearings. Gather her energy. As she'd packed her things at Goldmar, she'd ignored Steve's bleating about her needing to hand in the BMW. Given the stuff she'd put up with, she deserved at least a week's grace.

Deciding to make good use of the vehicle while she had it—and not wanting to think about dropping it off—she'd packed a few provisions and driven out to Tyler's Stream. Other than escape, she wasn't certain why she'd decided to head back to her hometown. When she'd arrived, however, it had dawned. She wanted to return as the person she was now and take the time to remember her mother in a different light...as a woman who'd fallen head over heels and had only wanted that love returned.

Boy, could she relate.

After arriving late last night, thankfully she'd fallen into a deep sleep and hadn't stirred until ten this morning. It was as if she'd completely run down and needed to recharge her batteries in readiness for the next phase of her life. Dragging herself out of her loft bed, she reminded herself of how strong she could be. Three months from now, surely the pain over losing Pace would have eased to almost bearable. She simply had to put one foot in front of the other and get on with it until then.

After showering, she dressed in low-waisted pants and a peasant top before catching her hair in a high ponytail. Convalescing here with lots of quiet and fresh air would be ideal. But only for a week, tops. Aunt Meg would be back soon, and Phoebe wanted to have accepted that position and be into her new role before her aunt had time to worry.

Picking at a meagre breakfast, she slid a glance around her lonely-looking cottage, remembering the amazing night she and Pace had spent here. The night she'd taken another stand and had stomped out, once and for all, those horrible, haunting insecurities. The smell of the slow-burning fire…that sultry music washing over her… She'd gone from nervous to curious to full-blown vamp in a matter of minutes.

Crossing to the kitchen, she dropped her dish in the sink.

That glorious night seemed a lifetime ago. Today she only smelled the damp of the previous day's rain and heard the wind picking up outside. She could light a fire, but a walk would clear her head and give her body the exercise and oxygen it needed. Deciding to pass on a coat, she called Hannie and they headed out.

Ten minutes later, strolling by the stream, Phoebe found a smile when her little dog bolted off, racing for Phoebe's special tree as its glossy clumps of leaves came into view. With a crisp chill in the air, she regretted passing on her coat. But the water's familiar fresh scent and soft babbling comforted her, and her mind wound back to a time when she'd known the perfume of cotton-wool blossoms floating all around.

Nearing the tree, she remembered, too, that secret, special time when she'd first carved her initials and a love heart into its trunk. She'd believed with all her soul that, no matter what, magic did exist: love didn't always desert you. Just a child, she'd even thought if she wished hard enough her mother would come back one day.

As a teenager, and more aware of her position— illegitimate, orphaned—her perception of reality and love had changed. After age thirteen she hadn't touched that carving again.

Now she reached into her back pocket. But, rather than a penknife, she found the folded sheet of paper she'd placed there before leaving her cottage.

Her wish list.

As the breeze played with her ponytail, she noted the points with a subjective eye—particularly the first. She'd wanted to find *Mr Right Now* and she had. Despite the pain of accepting they'd broken up for good, she simply couldn't regret her time with Pace. He'd been the catalyst behind her facing so much about herself. He'd helped her to grow. Indirectly, he'd helped her to forgive. For that, more than anything, she was grateful.

Phoebe held the list tight, shut her eyes, sent up a prayer that she stay strong, then tore the paper as many times as she could. She watched the pieces float away on the rising wind, her eyes edged with tears and her stomach sinking even lower.

What came next?

She could go full circle and try to believe that magic would find her again…but she couldn't imagine kissing anyone else, *loving* anyone else, other than Pace. No one could hold her the same way or bring out the unbridled joy he did. It wasn't so much about sex. It was about finding that one extraordinary connection. Discovering that unique person you could spend the rest of your life happily getting to know.

A knot in her chest, she brushed a tear aside, and she had begun to walk off when she paused to blink back over her shoulder. Hannie was running around in circles, yapping at the plump white blossoms that were drifting from the boughs up above. She frowned. Edged around. But that couldn't be. It wasn't spring. It was closer to winter—in more ways than one.

Shading her eyes, she spied a giant cardboard box nestled within the tree's nearest fork. A masculine hand reached in, and then a sprinkle of flowers whirled down from the branches, one handful after another. Before she had time to think it through, the box was upended to spill its entire contents, and Phoebe's world was transformed into a petal-filled wonderland. Through the tree's foliage a far more handsome version of a Cheshire Cat's smile appeared.

Her eyes widening, she held her throat.

Pace?

He'd swung down and landed before Phoebe could swallow. When he stepped close, he blocked off the wind and murmured in that lethally sexy voice, "Surprise."

A flicker of warmth lit in her chest at the same time as a smile hovered around her lips. But she had the presence of mind to tamp them down quickly. He hadn't so much as tried to call this past week. He'd got on with his life.

So had she.

She assembled her courage and met his gaze square-on. "What are you doing here?"

"I heard you gave Steve Trundy a mouthful and left Goldmar Studios. I wanted to say, good for you."

Her lips twisted into a cynical line. "You didn't come all the way down here to say that."

If he thought he could turn on the charm and seduce her back into his bed, he could think again. She loved him more than her soul, but she also respected herself—and in her book that was sacred. A knife in the heart might have hurt less than letting him go and then forcing herself not to crumple later or throw herself at his feet. But she'd done it. She wouldn't surrender now only to be passed over again when his next challenge came along.

He had no idea how low he'd made her feel that night.

How dispensable.

But he was looking at her now as if nothing else existed…as if he'd found his way out of a maze and she was the door. As his gaze combed her face, heat leapt up her neck to scorch her cheeks. He was as convincing as he'd ever been. Hypnotic. Fatally seductive.

She stood up tall.

She wasn't going there again.

"When I walked away that night," he said, stepping closer, "I thought it was best. I knew I had to work with my brother and get the company back up to speed. I was going to be busy. I *am* busy. You deserve someone who'll be there for you whenever you need him, one hundred percent."

A fist-sized ache swelled in her throat. What was this? Torture hour?

"Well, thanks for dropping in and clearing that up."

When he reached out, his hand settled on her forearm. Her first instinct was to sigh at the contact. His touch always felt so hot, so right. But she remembered her mother, and how bereft she'd felt the night Pace had walked away, and found the wherewithal to shirk back.

Pace's brows fell together. "Phoebe, we need to talk—"

"There's nothing left to say."

"You need to take a minute—"

"I need to get on with my life."

His chest expanded on a breath and his eyes narrowed, as though he were working something through in his mind. Then he reached for her arm again, more determined this time.

"We'll go back to your cottage, out of the weather and—"

Her heart pounding and breaking all over again,

she stepped back. "Whatever you have to say, Pace, please—just say it."

He studied her for a long moment, the intensity of his gaze rippling over her like heatwaves, those fake blossoms swirling all around. He might have come to apologise, but she hadn't been born yesterday. They were highly compatible together into the bedroom. He thought he could win that privilege back. He should have thought about that while he was living a double life. Before he'd let her know something more important had come up and he was bowing out of their relationship.

A breeze ruffled his dark hair as he slid his hands in his coat pockets.

"I was wrong, Phoebe. Dead wrong. That's hard for me to admit. Growing up, I always had to be right—or put on a good show that I was. Competing with my brother every step of the way…trying to make my father proud when most of the time I only ever felt overshadowed and overwhelmed by him. I wasn't ready to take on the head chair when he died. I should have asked for Nick's help then. But I was stubborn. The worst thing I could've done, or so I thought, was to show any weakness."

Phoebe frowned. But this man was confidence personified. She didn't know anyone who exuded more self-assurance than he did.

She shook her head. "That's ridiculous."

"As ridiculous as you needing to find 'Mr Right Now' to prove something to yourself." His hands eased from his pockets and took hers, so warm, so firm. "Don't you know that you're the most beautiful, desirable woman alive?"

A rush of hot emotion flooded her veins and a well of moisture rose in her eyes, but she held the tears back. She needed to keep her head and remember that this was *Pace*, the consummate flirter, bad boy and breaker of hearts. He'd go a long way to get what he wanted. Apparently even as far as pretending to open his heart.

When she tried to free her hands he released one, but held the other, unyielding.

Quivering inside—with anger, with desire—she raised her chin. "If you think you can sweet-talk me back because after a week your bed is cold—"

"This is me saying that you and I have a lot in common. Something very human. Everyone doubts themselves some time. No one likes to admit it. Who I am with you is the real me. Doesn't matter if it's Pace or Davis. I want to succeed in business like you want to succeed in your profession. But I want you more. So much more. I want to be with you. I think you want that too."

Couldn't he show some mercy and leave? Even if a world of magnets was pulling her towards him and deep inside a voice was telling her to succumb. To forgive.

"Pace, you have no idea what I want." *She* hardly knew any more.

"You want passion and fun." He stepped near and brought that palm to his lips. "You want love and commitment."

A warm tear trickled down her cheek; more lay aching in her throat. If he'd stooped to saying that simply to get her back in his bed, he'd gone too far.

She was about to tell him as much when, through blurred vision, something caught her eye. That tear curled around her chin at the same time as she recognised a dazzling gem glittering up from the crimson jewellery box Pace held. She shook her head, disbelieving, as he gathered her into a single-armed caress and brought the box higher.

"I was wrong," he said, his lips nuzzling the shell of her ear, his breath warming her cheek. "I should never have walked away."

His mouth trailed her brow and she swallowed hard against the want clutching at her heart and the urge to collapse and believe everything he'd said.

"This past week," he went on, "I've learned that you're the one person who makes it all real and clear and worthwhile for me. If you let yourself trust me again you'll admit that you love me the same way I love you."

A wave of emotion crashed and broke free. Smothering a hitched sob, she buried her face against his broad chest. Could she believe him? Had her father ever said that he'd loved her mother?

But Pace had a ring. A beautiful ring...the most beautiful ever created.

When he cupped her face she met his gaze, shamefully weak with hope.

"I can't wave a wand," he said. "Wish I could. I knew in my heart when we said goodbye that night I was making the biggest mistake of my life. I won't let you go again." His head lowered over hers. "Marry me, Phoebe," he whispered, his lips touching hers. "Be my wife, my partner. We'll ride on the good times and weather the bad. We'll do it together. And I promise we'll be happier than two people have a right to be."

When his mouth slanted over and captured hers,

Phoebe felt as if she were Aladdin opening that mysterious, wondrous cave. All those elusive treasures could be hers…

If she said yes.

If this was really for ever.

"I saw my life as win or lose," he said when they came up for air. "Wrong or right. It's not about that. It's about this."

He kissed her again, bringing her flush against him, and as her eyes drifted shut again all she could feel—all she could see—were those blossoms swirling around their heads and the magic breaking open in her heart. Then she was holding his face, too, her tears of happiness spilling freely. In her head those blossoms lit up like stars, and the answer—the *only* answer—seemed to light up and blaze in her mind too.

His chest rumbled as their lips parted. Rubbing the tip of his nose against hers, this time he didn't speak to her eyes. He spoke to her soul.

"I can be president of a company, and I can design a car." He smiled. "A damn good one. But what I want… what I need more than anything…is to spend my life with you. Don't let this past week get in the way of what we have."

She searched his eyes. "What *do* we have?"

"Phoebe…darling…we have each other."

Won over, she dropped her head back and waited for his kiss. She would have waited for ever, she thought. But when it didn't happen she slowly frowned and opened her eyes. One coal-black eyebrow was hiking up.

"Phoebe? Do you believe me?"

Her dawning smile was soft…was real.

"Yes," she sighed. "I believe you."

The groove disappeared from between his brows and a dazzling smile lit up his face. His voice deepened as he held her tighter. "Do you love me even half as much as I love you?"

"Much more than that." It seemed as if she'd always loved him.

"Then your answer's yes? You'll be my bride?"

A choked laugh escaped. "Tomorrow, if you want."

"Because, if you have any doubts, I can show you something I think might help."

He tilted his head towards the base of her tree and her gaze was drawn to the biggest knot—to the place where she'd etched her initials and that love heart so many years ago. A heartbeat before he drew her unequivocally close—before he sealed their once-in-a-lifetime love the way she liked best—Phoebe's heart swelled as she recognised the letters he'd carved above her own.

Davis Brodrick
loves
Phoebe Moore

Coming Next Month

from **Harlequin Presents®**. Available November 23, 2010.

Coming Next Month

from **Harlequin Presents® EXTRA.** Available December 7, 2010.

LARGER-PRINT
BOOKS!

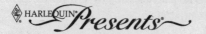

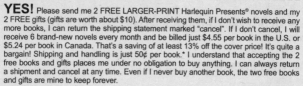

GET 2 FREE LARGER-PRINT
NOVELS PLUS 2 FREE GIFTS!

YES! Please send me 2 FREE LARGER-PRINT Harlequin Presents® novels and my 2 FREE gifts (gifts are worth about $10). After receiving them, if I don't wish to receive any more books, I can return the shipping statement marked "cancel". If I don't cancel, I will receive 6 brand-new novels every month and be billed just $4.55 per book in the U.S. or $5.24 per book in Canada. That's a saving of at least 13% off the cover price! It's quite a bargain! Shipping and handling is just 50¢ per book.* I understand that accepting the 2 free books and gifts places me under no obligation to buy anything. I can always return a shipment and cancel at any time. Even if I never buy another book, the two free books and gifts are mine to keep forever.

176/376 HDN E5NG

Name _____ (PLEASE PRINT) _____

Address _____ Apt. # _____

City _____ State/Prov. _____ Zip/Postal Code _____

Signature (if under 18, a parent or guardian must sign)

Mail to the **Harlequin Reader Service:**
IN U.S.A.: P.O. Box 1867, Buffalo, NY 14240-1867
IN CANADA: P.O. Box 609, Fort Erie, Ontario L2A 5X3

Not valid for current subscribers to Harlequin Presents Larger-Print books.

**Are you a subscriber to Harlequin Presents books
and want to receive the larger-print edition?
Call 1-800-873-8635 today!**

* Terms and prices subject to change without notice. Prices do not include applicable taxes. Sales tax applicable in N.Y. Canadian residents will be charged applicable provincial taxes and GST. Offer not valid in Quebec. This offer is limited to one order per household. All orders subject to approval. Credit or debit balances in a customer's account(s) may be offset by any other outstanding balance owed by or to the customer. Please allow 4 to 6 weeks for delivery. Offer available while quantities last.

Your Privacy: Harlequin Books is committed to protecting your privacy. Our Privacy Policy is available online at www.eHarlequin.com or upon request from the Reader Service. From time to time we make our lists of customers available to reputable third parties who may have a product or service of interest to you. ☐ If you would prefer we not share your name and address, please check here.

Help us get it right—We strive for accurate, respectful and relevant communications. To clarify or modify your communication preferences, visit us at www.ReaderService.com/consumerchoice.

HPLP10R

HARLEQUIN®

A Romance

FOR EVERY MOOD™

Spotlight on

Classic

Quintessential, modern love stories
that are romance at its finest.

See the next page
to enjoy a sneak peek from
the Harlequin® Romance series.

*See below for a sneak peek from our classic
Harlequin® Romance® line.*

Introducing DADDY BY CHRISTMAS by Patricia Thayer.

MIA caught sight of Jarrett when he walked into the open
lobby. It was hard not to notice the man. In a charcoal
business suit with a crisp white shirt and striped tie covered
by a dark trench coat, he looked more Wall Street than
small-town Colorado.

Mia couldn't blame him for keeping his distance. He
was probably tired of taking care of her.

Besides, why would a man like Jarrett McKane be
interested in her? Why would he want to take on a woman
expecting a baby? Yet he'd done so many things for her.
He'd been there when she'd needed him most. How could
she not care about a man like that?

Heart pounding in her ears, she walked up behind him.
Jarrett turned to face her. "Did you get enough sleep last
night?"

"Yes, thanks to you," she said, wondering if he'd thought
about their kiss. Her gaze went to his mouth, then she
quickly glanced away. "And thank you for not bringing up
my meltdown."

Jarrett couldn't stop looking at Mia. Blue was definitely
her color, bringing out the richness of her eyes.

"What meltdown?" he said, trying hard to focus on what
she was saying. "You were just exhausted from lack of
sleep and worried about your baby."

He couldn't help remembering how, during the night,
he'd kept going in to watch her sleep. How strange was
that? "I hope you got enough rest."

She nodded. "Plenty. And you're a good neighbor for

coming to my rescue."

He tensed. Neighbor? *What neighbor kisses you like I did?* "That's me, just the full-service landlord," he said, trying to keep the sarcasm out of his voice. He started to leave, but she put her hand on his arm.

"Jarrett, what I meant was you went beyond helping me." Her eyes searched his face. "I've asked far too much of you."

"Did you hear me complain?"

She shook her head. "You should. I feel like I've taken advantage."

"Like I said, I haven't minded."

"And I'm grateful for everything…"

Grasping her hand on his arm, Jarrett leaned forward. The memory of last night's kiss had him aching for another. "I didn't do it for your gratitude, Mia."

Gorgeous tycoon Jarrett McKane has never believed in Christmas—but he can't help being drawn to soon-to-be-mom Mia Saunders! Christmases past were spent alone…and now Jarrett may just have a fairy-tale ending for all his Christmases future!

Available December 2010, only from Harlequin® Romance®.

HARLEQUIN *Presents*

Bestselling Harlequin Presents® author

Julia James

brings you her most powerful book yet…

FORBIDDEN OR FOR BEDDING?

The shamed mistress…

Guy de Rochemont's name is a byword for wealth
and power—and now his duty is to wed.

Alexa Harcourt knows she can never be anything
more than *The de Rochemont Mistress.*

But Alexa—the one woman Guy wants—is also
the one woman whose reputation
forbids him to take her as his wife….

**Available from Harlequin Presents
December 2010**